"You should open a craft shop," he said.

"I don't want to run a craft shop."

"But yarn always sells. And quilting supplies. You'd always have a business."

"Jesse, you're being impossible!" Fannie said. "You know me—when have I ever been excited about quilting?"

Jesse shot her a grin. "You only need to sell the supplies, Fannie."

"I loved that bookstore." She sighed. "I spent hours in it as a girl. Your *daet* used to let me borrow books when I couldn't afford to buy them, and I'd read them in the back corner of the store. You know that."

"He was nicer to you than he was to me," Jesse muttered.

"I could escape in those books," she went on. "My life might not have been very exciting, but those books let me live a hundred different lives—they let me have adventures I'd never experience on my own. Your *daet* was a good man—"

"My *daet* was not a good man." Jesse cut her off, and fire blazed in his eyes.

Patricia Johns is a *Publishers Weekly* bestselling author who writes from Alberta, Canada, where she lives with her husband and son. She writes Amish romances that will leave you yearning for a simpler life. You can find her at patriciajohns.com and on social media, where she loves to connect with her readers. Drop by her website and you might find your next read!

Books by Patricia Johns

Love Inspired

Amish Chocolate Shop Brides

An Amish Baby in Her Arms
An Amish Bookshop Courtship

Amish Country Matches

The Amish Matchmaking Dilemma
Their Amish Secret
The Amish Marriage Arrangement
An Amish Mother for His Child
Her Pretend Amish Beau
Amish Sleigh Bells

Harlequin Heartwarming

An Amish Antiques Shop Romance

Her Amish Country Husband

Visit the Author Profile page at LoveInspired.com for more titles.

If you purchased this book without a cover you should be aware that this book is stolen property. It was reported as "unsold and destroyed" to the publisher, and neither the author nor the publisher has received any payment for this "stripped book."

ISBN-13: 978-1-335-23025-6

An Amish Bookshop Courtship

Copyright © 2025 by Patricia Johns

All rights reserved. No part of this book may be used or reproduced in any manner whatsoever without written permission.

Without limiting the author's and publisher's exclusive rights, any unauthorized use of this publication to train generative artificial intelligence (AI) technologies is expressly prohibited.

This is a work of fiction. Names, characters, places and incidents are either the product of the author's imagination or are used fictitiously. Any resemblance to actual persons, living or dead, businesses, companies, events or locales is entirely coincidental.

For questions and comments about the quality of this book, please contact us at CustomerService@Harlequin.com.

® is a trademark of Harlequin Enterprises ULC.

Love Inspired
22 Adelaide St. West, 41st Floor
Toronto, Ontario M5H 4E3, Canada
www.LoveInspired.com

HarperCollins Publishers
Macken House, 39/40 Mayor Street Upper,
Dublin 1, D01 C9W8, Ireland
www.HarperCollins.com

Printed in U.S.A.

Recycling programs for this product may not exist in your area.

AN AMISH BOOKSHOP COURTSHIP

PATRICIA JOHNS

House and riches are the inheritance of fathers:
and a prudent wife is from the Lord.
—*Proverbs* 19:14

To my husband and our son. I love you both.
You're the center of my world.

Chapter One

Jesse Kauffman stood in the middle of his late father's bookstore and scanned the cramped, cluttered shop. There were books that appealed to Amish and Englishers alike in this store. The shelves were packed with books, and stacks of them were piled up in the back room, waiting for space to be displayed. There was Christian fiction, books on nature, tomes on church history. Amish folks could buy German Luther Bibles—new ones meant to last for generations. Jesse's grandfather had one such Bible, and it was two hundred years old, passed down from father to son all the way back to Switzerland. They had a stock of hymnbooks, too, still covered in cellophane. Those were popular—they got used a lot, and damaged over time. Englisher tourists had always liked the big, glossy paged books that showed aerial views of Amish Country—just none with photos of Amish folks in them. Jesse's *daet*, Caleb Kauffman, had been particular about that.

Jesse picked up a pile of dusty postcards. They showed some Amish scenes—a buggy passing by on one, cattle grazing on another. His father hadn't let him play with those when he was a boy. He'd been forbidden. Jesse put them back. His throat felt tight. His *daet* had died six weeks ago, and the memories were thick and stifling in this shop.

Someone tapped on the door, and Jesse sighed. He'd been turning away customers all day—locals and tourists alike who wanted to come browse in Kauffman Books. He wasn't here to sell anything. He was shutting it all down for good. He muttered under his breath as he pulled the door open for the tenth time that morning.

"We're closed—" he said started to say, but he stopped short.

A young woman stood at the door, a thick shawl wrapped around her shoulders and her feet in a pair of felt-lined boots. She wore a black bonnet over her head, and her shoulders were hunched up against the cold, glittering gray eyes meeting his.

"Hi, Jesse."

"Fannie..." He hadn't seen Fannie Flaud in two years, and when they'd last parted, it had been complicated. "Uh—come in." He stepped back, and she slipped past him into the shop. She stomped the snow off her boots, and he shut the door behind her, the overhead bell tinkling.

He looked up at it. He hated that bell.

"You didn't come by to see me when you got back in town?" Fannie said. "Esther Mae told me that you were over here, and that was the first I heard of it."

Esther Mae was the owner of Black Bonnet Amish Chocolates, which was located across the street from the bookshop, and she'd been one of the people who'd tapped on the door that morning.

"I was going to...later," Jesse said. "I'm sorry, Fannie. It's great to see you. It really is."

She eyed him, her lips pursed. "You didn't write, either. Two years you've been away, and I don't even have an address to write to you. What if there was news?"

If something had happened, his grandparents would have written. But that wasn't the kind of answer Fannie was looking for.

"Look, when I left, your *ankel* and my *daet* were trying to—"

"I know!" She threw her hands up. "But that wasn't me! You didn't even bother to ask me if I wanted it. Do you think I wanted to be pushed into marrying my best friend?"

Did she? He wasn't sure, so he just looked at her. Fannie rolled her eyes.

"I didn't, if you needed that spelled out. So I hope you feel absolutely terrible about not even bothering to write."

She crossed her arms over her chest and met his gaze with that defiant stare of hers that brought a smile to his lips. She was the same old Fannie, and he felt a surge of relief.

Jesse swallowed. "Fannie, when I left two years ago, I had determined that I wasn't coming back to Menno Hills. My grandfather contacted me and said I had to come back and deal with Daet's shop for the inheritance. I wasn't going to even bother with that much, but if I didn't, I was leaving a big burden for everyone else."

"Oh." Fannie straightened, her jaw tensing. He could tell that he was offending her. The truth could do that sometimes. He wasn't back home for a happy Christmas visit. This was an obligation.

"I just mean that—" Jesse heaved a sigh. "Look, I'm not staying long, either. My grandparents want me to stay for Christmas, and my carpentry job in Indiana is shut down until the new year, so I said I would stay that long. But then I'm leaving again—for good. So, that's why I didn't write, or come find you right away.

I figured you'd probably yell at me—or whatever the equivalent is in a letter."

"*Yah*, I might have," Fannie agreed. "But I'm not here to talk you out of your decisions."

"No?" he asked cautiously.

"I'm here to ask you for a favor." She looked up at him hopefully. "I need you to ask me to go driving with you tonight."

"What?" Jesse squinted at her. When men asked women to go driving, there was a very pointed reason for that. That would be seen as courting. "I thought we agreed that—"

"Please! As my friend, nothing more. I wouldn't ask anything of you if it weren't incredibly important. But my *ankel* has lined up another eligible match for me, and I need to be out of the house by seven at the latest. And I need to be gone for a couple of hours." Fannie's eyes blazed. "Just ask—"

"Uh…can I take you driving tonight?" he said.

"*Danke*…" Fannie's shoulders lowered and she gave him a grateful nod. "Now, when I tell my uncle I can't meet that farmer, I will be telling the honest truth. What time can you pick me up? The earlier the better. I don't want to be available for any introductions. Besides, my *ankel* liked you enough to suggest I marry you, so I'm sure they'll like the idea of us spending time together. So long as I'm with you, I think they'll give me the space I need to sort out my future."

This sounded like her *ankel* was up to the same old trick—trying to get Fannie married. And it would seem that Fannie didn't like his choice.

"What farmer?" Jesse asked.

Fannie loosened her bonnet and removed it, placing it on the counter next to the till. She rubbed her hands together and moved toward the potbellied stove, holding her palms outward toward the heat. Her fingernails were chewed down to the quick. It looked like she hadn't broken that habit yet.

"He's a widower from another community," Fannie explained. "He's almost forty and has five little *kinner* who need a new *mamm*. My *ankel* set up a meeting, and I know what everyone is wanting. Obviously, they want me married and provided for."

Fannie's parents had passed away five years earlier, and she'd moved in with her uncle and aunt from her father's side.

"How terrible," he said ruefully. "To get married and have a home of your own, a kitchen of your own—"

"It's not terrible on the surface," she said, cutting him off. "But I don't want to marry a man who's almost as old as my *daet*. I don't want to be a stepmother to five *kinner*! That's a lot to ask. I'm twenty-two."

He sobered.

"Besides," she went on, "Ankel Moe is getting ready to sell up and retire. He and Aent Bethany want to go to Florida with my other *aents* who settled out there."

"And you aren't going," Jesse guessed.

"Of course not," she replied. "My parents are buried here. My friends and cousins and whole community are here. And going to Florida is expensive. I have a feeling that getting me married and provided for is part of their retirement plan. I'm in the way, Jesse."

"And you really don't like this widower?" Jesse asked.

"I'm not interested."

Jesse hated the rush of relief that flooded through him. He had no right to it. She was a friend—one he'd left in his past, at that. But *gut*! She shouldn't be marrying some widower almost twice her age. He hated that idea, too.

"You'll have to tell Moe that you don't want to marry the man," Jesse said. "And that'll be the end of it."

"Not exactly." She pressed her lips together. "They seem to think I'll be hard to match up. They're seeming a little desperate on my behalf.

If it isn't this older farmer, it'll be someone else they dig up, and probably someone less appealing still. I need some time to figure out a way to support myself, and until I do that, I need them to stop trying to foist me off on some widower in want of a wife. I just need them to give me space until, say…after Christmas."

Fannie cast him a hopeful look, and Jesse could feel the real request coming.

"And you need…?"

"I need a single man of appropriate age to spend time with me," she said in a practical tone of voice. "I need him to act like he's interested. If they think an eligible man is interested in me, they'll leave me alone for a while, and it will give me time to think. I have to look into renting a room somewhere, and cobbling together an income for myself. I need *time*!"

This was the Fannie he remembered. She was whip-smart and absolutely refused to be coerced into anything. And he hated the thought of anyone pushing her around. She should marry a nice fellow when she loved him, and not a moment sooner.

"And this single man of appropriate age…" Jesse crossed his arms over his chest and met her gaze with a small smile. "Have you found one?"

"You?" she asked hopefully. That sound in

her voice—the soft pleading. It was his weakness. "I know this timing is terrible. But they liked you enough to try and match us up before. I think they'd like the idea, and they'd leave me alone. I can even tell them that I'm supporting you through the loss of your *daet*—"

"I don't need that," he said, and turned back toward the stove again. "I'm sorting out his death in my own way."

He was pushing it into the back of his mind and dismantling this shop that was so full of unpleasant memories. He wasn't grieving—he was moving past it.

"Okay..." she murmured.

But Jesse knew how his return to Menno Hills looked, especially since he hadn't returned for his *daet*'s funeral six weeks ago, either. He did have things to sort out inside of himself, but it wasn't the grief everyone assumed.

"You want me to act interested and shoo off any suitors you don't like for the next couple of weeks?" Jesse asked.

"If you don't mind. There should only be the one." She shrugged weakly. "They don't line up for me."

She'd always had a self-deprecating sense of humor that had made him laugh, but there was something rather sad in that statement. They didn't line up for her. Well, they should. Fannie was a better cook, a more loyal friend, a better seamstress—she was worth their time.

"Okay, I can do that...and maybe in return you can help me pack things up here," Jesse said.

"Of course!" She brightened.

Besides, Jesse had thought he wanted to clean out Kauffman Books alone and marinate in his frustrated memories, but maybe the job would be less miserable with some company. Well, with Fannie's company, to be more specific. Fannie understood him best, and she'd always been levelheaded. Besides, seeing her again, he realized how much he'd missed her.

"Maybe we can help each other out," Jesse agreed. "For old times' sake."

"*Danke*," she said, and looked out the window. "Esther Mae said she'd drive me home today, so I have to get back to the shop. I don't want to hold her up. I work again first thing tomorrow morning."

"Do you want a ride to work tomorrow?" Jesse asked. "That could start a few rumors in your favor."

Fannie shot him a grin. "That would be perfect. And I need you to pick me up at seven tonight for a long drive. I'll treat you to pizza here in town to make it up to you."

"Deal." He wouldn't let her pay, but that was an argument for later.

"Are you going to enjoy this at all?" she asked.

"Helping you dodge a dismal marriage to an older farmer? It sounds downright fun. Prepare yourself for a very public courting, Fannie Flaud." He shot her a mischievous grin.

Fannie eyed him uncertainly, and he chuckled. It would be the best part of this miserable trip. At least he'd get some time with Fannie before he put Menno Hills behind him for good.

Later that afternoon in the Black Bonnet Amish Chocolates shop, Fannie stood to the side, her shawl wrapped around her tightly, waiting as Esther Mae gathered up her purse and pulled on her gloves. Another worker, Iris Bischel, would run the chocolate shop for the last two hours before she closed up for the evening at seven. There were always the after-work customers, and the tourists who liked to walk the streets of Menno Hills after dinner out.

Fannie looked out the big display window. She could see Kauffman Books across the street—the inside lit up with a kerosene lamp. Jesse was still there, and her heart pattered in her throat. Jesse was back…and while she pretended it wasn't a big deal, it was. She'd missed him more than she would ever admit to his face. He didn't know about that.

The Englisher shops along the main street

were twinkling with lights and Christmas decorations this time of year, but Amish shops kept things plain. Black Bonnet Amish Chocolates had some boxed chocolates on display, and there were some evergreen sprigs and linen ribbons used to decorate, but that was all. The meaning of Christmas was not in the baubles and glitz that the Englishers loved so much—it was about Jesus coming to this earth as a tiny, crying newborn.

Esther Mae, the owner of the shop, was giving Iris Bischel a few last-minute instructions about some chocolate orders to be picked up. One had already been paid for, but a second order hadn't been. Iris was in her late thirties, and she'd never married. Fannie wondered if she would end up like Iris. It wouldn't be bad—when Iris wasn't working at the chocolate shop, she was coaching girls' volleyball at the community center. She was beloved by Amish and Englishers alike.

"I think that's everything. Thank you, Iris," Esther Mae said.

"It's no problem at all," Iris said with a smile. "Have a good night."

Fannie and Esther Mae headed out of the shop just as some customers went in, and Fannie held the door for them. She looked across the street at Kauffman Books once more. There was still a light shining inside, and a shadow passed the front window. She squinted. It was Jesse. He stopped and raised one hand, and her heart skipped a beat. She waved back, hoping the heat in her cheeks didn't mean she was blushing.

"I'm glad to see that boy back home," Esther Mae said, leading the way back round the building toward the stable where the horses were kept during the day. "So sad about his father's death, though. People talked when Jesse didn't come back for the funeral, but everyone grieves differently. He must have just needed time."

The women hitched up Esther Mae's buggy quickly between the two of them, the wind whipping Fannie's skirt and her fingers fumbling with the buckles and straps. The temperature was dropping, and they gave Iris's horse some extra grain and another blanket over his back before they closed up the stable against the prying cold, and got up into the buggy.

"You must be glad to see Jesse, too," Esther Mae said as she flicked the reins.

No one else knew about the plan to arrange a marriage between them, thankfully. At least that embarrassment wasn't public.

"*Yah*, I really am," Fannie agreed. "I missed him."

That was too much to reveal right now, but it had just come out of her mouth. She tended to be honest to a fault that way.

"Will you see more of him?" Esther Mae asked.

"Definitely." Fannie shot her boss a smile. "He's taking me driving tonight."

"Oh my!" Esther Mae's eyebrows went up. "It seems he missed you, too."

Fannie didn't want to say much more because she didn't want to lie or tell too much of the truth, but it was nice to think that in a few short hours she'd be out driving with her old friend again. Fannie wasn't the only single woman in Menno Hills, though. Esther Mae had been married a very long time ago, and he'd passed away. No one seemed to be finding her a new marriage, though. That hardly seemed fair.

"Esther Mae, how come no one is trying to set you up with another husband?" Fannie asked.

"Me?" Esther Mae looked surprised. "I've already been married once. That's enough for me."

"And everyone just accepts that?" Fannie asked.

"I've been widowed now for fifteen years," she replied. "It took time, but eventually the community gave up on matching me."

"How long did it take?" Fannie asked.

"Three or four years, I think," Esther Mae said, and she cast Fannie a cautious look. "Why do you ask?"

"Just curious."

Three or four years... That was a long time

to dodge well-intentioned setups. But she didn't blame her *ankel* and *aent* for wanting to help her get started in a home of her own, especially when they were wanting to relocate to be closer to other extended family.

She'd simply have to find a way to support herself to put their minds at ease.

"Do you think you might be able to hire me on full-time?" Fannie asked.

"I don't have the hours to give you," Esther Mae said. "I wish I did. I'm sorry."

"It's okay..."

There had to be solutions. The canning factory paid a decent amount, but getting in full-time there was tough. They were laying off more than they were hiring right now—a few of the men in the community had lost their jobs recently. In the summer there was always need for local tour guides, but that was very seasonal.

The rest of the drive home, Fannie's mind spun through the possible jobs she might get that would help her to support herself. Esther Mae chatted about family news—her nephew who'd just gotten married to Miriam Smucker and the baby girl they'd adopted—and Fannie wondered how she could manage to create a full and happy life for herself like Esther Mae. There had to be a way!

When Esther Mae dropped her off, Fannie

thanked her for the ride and hopped out into the brisk, winter wind.

"Jesse will drive me to work tomorrow," Fannie called back into the buggy. "So I won't need the ride."

"Well, now!" Esther Mae shot her a smile. "I'll see you at the shop, then. Have a good night, Fannie."

Fannie hurried toward the side door as Esther Mae's buggy started to pull around and head back up to the snowy road. Fannie kicked the snow off her boots on the steps on her way up to the side door, then pushed open the door and headed inside. The house was warm and toasty, and Fannie gratefully pushed the door shut behind her. The kitchen smelled of cabbage rolls, and a roasting pan sat on top of the big, black kitchen stove, the lid open. Aent Bethany was peeling the protective cabbage leaves off the top of the pan to reveal the soft, tomato sauce–smothered rolls beneath.

"You're home!" Aent Bethany said, casting a smile over her shoulder. "Hello, Fannie. Maybe you could help me get that schnitz pie into the oven. I was hoping to have a nice warm pie waiting for when Dieter Glick arrives. I've put it all together, but we both know you make pie just as good as mine, so as long as you put the top crust on and slide it into the oven, we can call it yours."

Aent Bethany was a round woman with a round face and perpetually pink cheeks. Tonight, she wore her best blue dress, and a wide, white cooking apron that would protect her dress from the worst. She wiped her hand on the front of her apron and cast Fannie a sparkling smile. Her *aent*'s excitement was palpable.

Fannie hung her shawl on a peg by the door and put her stiff, black bonnet on the shelf above the pegs. She stepped out of her boots and into a pair of slippers. She rubbed her chilled hands together and headed for the sink to wash them.

"About Dieter Glick's visit," Fannie said, as she turned on the warm water and put a pump of soap into her hand. "I won't be here this evening."

"What do you mean?" Her aunt spun around. "Fannie, he's coming to see you."

"He didn't say that specifically," Fannie said.

"It's understood. He doesn't have to say it outright. That would be a little...brazen. But he's coming to visit with your *ankel* and see you. Maybe chat with you a little bit, and sample your good baking. Moe has been telling him what a decent and good young woman you are. And Dieter was asking questions about you."

Was she good with *kinner*? How was her cooking? How long ago had she taken the step of getting baptized into the faith? *Yah*, they'd already told her about Dieter's questions that her *aent* and *ankel* had found very encouraging indeed.

"Jesse Kauffman has asked me to go driving with him tonight," Fannie said. "And I said yes."

"Jesse Kauffman?" Her aunt stopped short. "Oh, Fannie..."

"I thought you liked him!"

"We did like him. We do like him...but last time we even suggested a match between the two of you, he up and left town. He didn't give you any warning. He didn't say good-bye. He marched out without a glance behind him. It was cruel and his actions spoke much louder than words. You didn't deserve that treatment."

Her aunt was right, of course. Fannie had been stunned and heartbroken. What she'd believed was a strong and enduring friendship had simply cracked apart when Jesse left town. And he'd never written to explain, either. If she were really looking for a marriage match, Jesse was a red flag. But she wasn't looking for marriage— she was looking for some space to think.

"He's a dear friend, and I'm glad to see him again," Fannie said. That was a true statement—no lie there.

Aent Bethany planted her hands on her ample hips. "If he's such a dear friend, then he'll be happy for you that you've got a possible marriage match, dear girl. These things don't come by every day."

Not for Fannie. Aent Bethany would never say such a thing, but Fannie knew it to be true. And Fannie noted that Aent Bethany hadn't even asked if Jesse was taking her out romantically, which was just a little bit deflating.

"I've already given my word to Jesse," Fannie said. "He's coming by to collect me at seven."

"And what about Dieter?"

"I haven't exchanged two words with the man, let alone promised him my time," Fannie said. "I'm sorry, Aent Bethany. I am. But I told Ankel Moe I didn't want to be introduced to Dieter as a potential match. That hasn't changed."

"And we respect that," Aent Bethany said. "We're introducing you to him as our niece. That's all. But it's such a good opportunity. He's a very kind man."

Kind enough to take on a plain-faced young woman who had no *kinner* of her own and could take on the wifely chores around his farm two church districts over. Kind. Not exciting. Not fun. Not full of potential. No, he was a man who already had five *kinner*, was undoubtedly still mourning the loss of his recently deceased wife, and needed a new wife rather quickly, and so wasn't inclined to be overly picky. Dieter Glick had already had a first marriage with all the excitement and romance that came with two young people falling in love and starting a family. Why was it so impossible for Fannie's family to understand that she didn't want to be a man's second wife while he was still mourning the first? If she married, she wanted that first marriage, first love, the first-time-for-everything experience.

The side door opened with a rush of cold air, and Ankel Moe came inside. He banged the door shut and stamped the snow off his boots.

"Fannie made plans this evening!" Aent Bethany said.

"Plans?" Ankel Moe dropped his hat on the shelf next to Fannie's bonnet. "But tonight Dieter Glick is coming to meet her."

Fannie licked her lips. "Ankel Moe, Jesse Kauffman has asked me to go driving with him."

Her uncle frowned. "Driving? As in...*driving*?"

He was making the connection now, and Fannie smiled. "I haven't seen him in a long time, and I told him I would go. He's collecting me at seven."

Ankel Moe and Aent Bethany exchanged a somber look.

"What will you tell Dieter?" Aent Bethany asked.

"I don't know." Moe turned back to Fannie. "Are you sure you can't ask Jesse to come tomorrow?"

Fannie shook her head. "*Nee*, Ankel."

Moe sighed. "You're a grown woman now. You can choose who you spend time with, but as your *ankel* I can give you some advice, Fannie. There are two kinds of men—the solid kind who stay, and the kind who leave when things get difficult. I know what kind of man Dieter is, and he's the solid kind a woman can count on. What kind is Jesse?"

Jesse Kauffman wasn't an ideal romantic match, but he was a loyal friend who would help her out of a bind when she asked him point-blank after two years of silence. He'd help her get the space she needed to find some solutions, and that was more than anyone else was doing for her right now.

"It's been a long time since Jesse left, and we're glad to see each other again. And I know him better than most. Jesse can be counted on," Fannie said.

In a different kind of way, perhaps, but he was trustworthy, nonetheless.

Chapter Two

Jesse pushed his plate back. He'd been hungrier than he thought when he got back from the bookstore that evening, and his grandmother had a huge meal ready for him. His grandfather only ate half a plateful, and Mammi just kept on dishing more onto Jesse's plate until he was completely stuffed. Back in Indiana, Jesse rented a room from another family, and no matter how kind and well-intentioned his landlady was, she'd never fed him like his Mammi did. A *mammi* measured portions with her heart, and the more she loved her grandson, the more she made him eat.

Mammi had outdone herself with dinner that night. She'd cooked a pork shoulder and scalloped potatoes, with pickled carrots and cauliflower on the side. Mammi had put some evergreen sprigs on the windowsills with some white pillar candles—her concession to Christmas decorating for Jesse's sake.

Dawdie bowed his head for the end-of-meal silent prayer, and Jesse bowed his head, too.

Gott, get me through this Christmas, Jesse prayed silently.

When his grandfather cleared his throat, indicating the prayer was over, Jesse pushed his chair back with a scrape, but Mammi and Dawdie exchanged a look.

"Before you go, there was something we wanted to discuss with you," Mammi said. "Something we feel is very important."

Jesse sank back into his seat. Here it was—the judgment that he knew was coming. He may even deserve it.

"Oh?" Jesse said, and he flicked his gaze over to his grandfather, who sat in stoic silence, his hands folded over his belly and his expression solemn. Dawdie had always looked gruffer and sterner than he really was—unlike Jesse's *daet*, who had been even worse than he looked.

"It's about your inheritance of the bookstore," Mammi went on. "Are you sure you want to sell Kauffman Books? We know your father wanted you to run it. He worked hard to build up that business and he wanted to leave it to you so you could support yourself. A fully established business is a greater gift than you might appreciate."

"I am supporting myself," Jesse replied. "I'm

working for a good furniture company in Indiana."

"You're working for someone else, though," Dawdie said. "You have your own business you can run here. The bookstore."

Dawdie's solemn expression didn't change. He was similar in mannerism to Daet, except Dawdie had never raised a hand to Jesse. But the sternness—however mild—was there, and Jesse found that old anger rising up inside of him in response to it.

"I know how hard Daet's death has been for you both," Jesse said, and his voice felt tight. "But the store is mine, and I need to do what is best for my own future. I'm not running that shop."

Dawdie's brows furrowed, and he pursed his lips.

"Isn't it best to keep it?" Mammi pressed, her gentleness in direct opposition to Dawdie's open displeasure. "Once you sell it, it can't be undone. It's the last gift your father can give you."

And that was the part that his grandparents couldn't understand—he didn't want any parting gifts from his father. Daet had spent Jesse's childhood being gruff, stern and an incredibly strict disciplinarian. His mother died when he was very young, and he hardly remembered her, so after his sisters married and left home when he was little, there was no softer presence. His father's discipline always happened behind doors. Never where anyone else could see. And the community had seen Jesse's good behavior as evidence of excellent parenting on his father's part, but it was far from the truth. Jesse's good behavior had been part fear and part choice. He'd wanted to be a good man because he wanted to be a good Christian. But he'd also been scared of ever crossing his father, lest his father whip him again.

"I live in Indiana now," Jesse countered.

"You could just as easily live here," Dawdie said. "You're renting a room. You haven't bought land, have you?"

"*Nee*, Dawdie, I haven't bought land."

"So you have some flexibility," his grandfather said. He still had a face like a thundercloud, but his words were gentler than his appearance. Jesse had often wondered why it was that his *daet* had been such a cruel, cold man when his *dawdie* had been kind to his very core, even if his expressions were stormy.

"I have decided to build my life in Indiana," Jesse said, choosing his words more carefully.

"But you could choose to come home," Mammi said softly. "We do miss you, Jesse. You don't have any family in Indiana, but you do have family here."

"Once I get my own place, you can visit me," Jesse said.

"It's harder to travel at our age," Dawdie said. "When your old bones hurt, sitting on a train or on a bus can leave you mighty sore. We don't unbend quite so easily as we used to."

They could do this all night—argue about where he lived, and why he chose it. And they'd argue for why he should come back. But Jesse didn't want to tell them the honest truth, that the memories he had from Menno Hills left him angry and bitter, and even though his *daet* was buried in the old Amish graveyard, those feelings were still fresh and alive. Jesse left Pennsylvania because he couldn't stand living here for another day. He was not moving back.

Jesse looked at the clock on the wall. It was nearly a quarter past six, and he'd promised to pick up Fannie at seven.

"I know this is important to talk about," Jesse said, "but do you think we could talk about this another time? I've got plans this evening, and I really don't want to be late."

"Plans?" Mammi's white eyebrows rose. "Are you seeing friends?"

"I'm taking Fannie Flaud out for a drive," he said.

Mammi's gaze snapped over to Dawdie, and even his gruff old grandfather looked pleasantly surprised to hear that.

A smile touched Mammi's weathered face. "Fannie is a wonderful girl."

"I agree." Jesse pushed back his chair. "Let me help you clear the table, and then I'll head out."

"You don't think you owe us a conversation about the bookstore?" Dawdie asked, raising his gaze to drill into Jesse.

"We'll talk about it later on, Dawdie. I promise." There would be no getting around it. "But Fannie is expecting me at seven." He looked over at the kitchen clock. "I don't have much time."

"Fine," Dawdie muttered.

"I'm glad you're spending time with Fannie again," Mammi said. "I always liked her."

This pretend courtship would help Fannie defer some marriage arrangements, but it looked like it would be helpful for Jesse, too. As long as he was focused on something his grandparents approved of, like finding a wife, they'd give him some space, too. It might be grudging on his grandfather's side, but it would be space nonetheless. And when Christmas was past, he was going back to Indiana where he could breathe, no matter how much his grandparents disapproved.

Jesse's heart was in a knot as he drove down the familiar old roads toward the Flaud place. This was why he'd stayed away. He looked like an unfeeling son, selfish, spoiled... But none of that was true. His grandparents had never believed him when he told them that his father treated him severely. Maybe it was because Daet had never been severe with his two older sisters. Only with Jesse, because he was going to be a man one day, and Daet said he needed to "man up now." His grandparents just said that a father needed to correct his children to protect them from dangerous mistakes. Mind, he hadn't told them the details, just that his *daet* was harsh. Maybe he should have spelled it out for them—outlined exactly what his *daet* was doing.

What his father had done was not *correcting*. Jesse pushed back the memories, but that heavy, anxious feeling stayed in the pit of his stomach. That was the feeling he was trying to escape, and the feeling that he'd be very glad to put behind him again when he left Menno Hills.

His grandparents loved him—he knew that. Even gruff old Dawdie loved him. But they would never hear a word said against their late son, Caleb. With his death, he became untouchable, and Jesse didn't even blame them for that. They hadn't seen what Jesse had seen, and now that Daet was dead, all they had were their memories. Jesse could appreciate how very painful that would be. But Jesse's experience of his father had been different, and he was tired of pretending otherwise.

The evening was crisp and cold, but the moon was bright, and the clouds had passed so that the silvery splash of moonlight sparkled over the snow-encrusted fields. Cattle herded closer together around feeders, hay and alfalfa trampled under their hooves. It was the kind of night a week before Christmas when a man couldn't help but start thinking about stables and shepherds and stars.

The stars were bright that night, too, and the familiar constellations created their patterns across the sky. The Big Dipper, the Little Dipper, and Orion with his three-starred belt. But a long time ago, there had been an extra star in the sky that had pointed to wonders about to unfold. And in dismal, frustrating times like these, Jesse couldn't help but yearn for some hope of his own.

The Flaud farm was located a few miles from Jesse's grandparents' acreage, and by the time he got there, Fannie came out the side door in a burst. She was wrapped up in her shawl and had thick mittens on her hands, and a big cloth bag with something heavy inside. That would be her bottles of hot water.

"Am I on time?" Jesse asked as she hoisted the bag up into the buggy first. He grabbed it and pulled it inside, and Fannie hopped up after it. She slammed the door shut, and he waited while she got settled. He tossed a thick woolen lap blanket over her legs, and Fannie arranged a bottle of hot water at her own feet, then pushed one next to his.

"Don't be a hero, Jesse," she said. "Just use the blanket."

He shot her a rueful smile and covered his own lap with the second blanket, the heat from the bottle snugged inside next to his legs. It did make a big difference, and on a long drive, the extra heat was a must.

Jesse leaned forward and looked out the window toward the house. Her *aent* and *ankel* were both at the window, and Bethany pulled back right away, but Moe just crossed his arms and met Jesse's gaze.

"Your *ankel* is suspicious," Jesse said, and he flicked the reins. "What happened with your farmer?"

"He's not my farmer," Fannie replied. "And he's coming by tonight. He hasn't arrived yet, though."

Jesse shot Fannie a rueful look. It felt good to be with her again, bantering and chatting like they used to do. And he was glad he'd gotten her out of there before that widower arrived. He knew nothing about the man, but he liked to think of Fannie free and happy like he remembered her, not encumbered with a marriage she didn't want. That thought grated at him in a way he couldn't ignore.

The horse plodded up the drive and they turned on to the road. Jesse leaned forward and took one last look back at the house, the light from the windows shining warmly into the night. The buggy shut out the wind, but the night was still cold. His fingertips were already getting chilled through his gloves, and he flexed his hands to get the blood moving.

"Scoot closer," Jesse said. "It's cold out tonight."

Fannie shuffled her hot-water bottle on the buggy floor and then slid closer to him until their blanket-swathed knees touched and she settled in against his arm. He could feel his heartbeat slowing to a steady, calm rhythm with her so close. Fannie made the world feel safer, somehow.

"Ankel Moe isn't pleased that I'm going out," Fannie said.

That was because they had another man all lined up for her. But Jesse couldn't help but feel a little offended that he'd be such miserable news as to have her *ankel* standing at the window like that. Jesse had been Moe's choice for Fannie two years ago, and now Moe didn't trust him?

"Did Moe forbid you?" Jesse asked.

"No, I'm a grown woman now," Fannie replied. "He can't very well forbid me, but he wanted me to stay."

"*Yah*, I know that feeling." He gave her a faint smile. "I dodged an uncomfortable conversation with my grandparents by coming to pick you up."

"And what is the 'uncomfortable conversation' about?" she asked.

"The bookshop."

"What about the bookshop?"

"I'm selling it."

Her eyes widened. "What? You're selling Kauffman Books? Why would you do that?"

"Because I don't want it," he said, his old stubborn gruffness rising up inside of him again. He was tired of trying to explain this. His deeper reasons weren't attractive. They were ugly, wounded and personal. "My life is in Indiana now, and I'm not keeping the shop. I want it sold as quickly as possible."

He spotted a buggy coming their way at a steady trot. There was something about the way the man was driving that told Jesse this was a man with a mission. He was illumined by the light of his headlamps, and he looked relatively fit, and he had a full, dark beard, which meant he was either married, or had been.

Jesse nodded at the man—he wasn't familiar—and the man nodded back. Jesse leaned forward as he passed and watched in his sideview mirror as the buggy slowed to turn down the Flauds' drive.

"That was your farmer," he said.

There had to be something wrong with the man, didn't there? Because just on that one glance, a tickle of dislike wormed up inside of him. This was the man they wanted for Fannie? No, Fannie could do better. Jesse was sure of it.

Fannie leaned forward to look in the sideview mirror, too, but she couldn't make out much, just the bob of some lights as they turned off the main road. That was her drive, wasn't it? That very likely was Dieter Glick. But if it was, he'd come without his *kinner*. She wasn't sure what that meant...but it was a near miss.

"Do you think that's him?" Fannie asked.

"Unless your uncle is expecting some other visitor tonight," he replied.

Fannie leaned back against the seat, her heartbeat taking a moment to settle down again.

"Do you have a girlfriend in Indiana?" she asked.

"Nee."

"Why not?"

"Why don't you have a boyfriend?" he countered.

"Because the boys my age chose other girls, and I didn't find someone who made my heart skip a beat."

"Like your *mamm* told you."

"You remembered that?" she asked.

Before her parents died in the buggy accident, her home had been full of life and laughter. Her older brothers had already moved away and started their own families, and Fannie had been her parents' surprise baby later in life. Much like Jesse had been with his family. Her *mamm* had been mistaken for her grandmother quite often, but she'd been full of advice and sparkling laughter.

"I remember you telling me about it. She told you that when she met your *daet*, her heart skipped a beat, and every day with him felt like the first day of summer."

"*Yah*...she said that." Fannie looked out the window at the bare trees, laden down with a fresh snowfall. "But that doesn't answer why you're still single."

"I'm new there," he said.

"And?" She shrugged. "You're new there! That's a good thing. You aren't related to half the available women. You're new and exciting. That should go in your favor, Jesse."

He cast her a rueful look and didn't answer. Maybe she'd embarrassed him.

"Maybe you shouldn't wait for skipped heartbeats and eternal sunshine," Jesse said.

"Why shouldn't I?" she asked.

"Some people would say it isn't realistic."

"My parents found it."

And her parents had been very happy together. They encouraged each other, and laughed at each other's jokes. They enjoyed each other's company. While it could be hard to tell who was married to who at a church event, Fannie's parents had always found a way to come talk to each other, or they'd exchange a smile between the women's side of the service and the men's.

"*Yah*, I know..." He sounded sad then.

"Your *mamm* and *daet* might have been just as happy," she added. Jesse's *mamm* had died when he was a toddler, and his *daet* had never remarried. But while they'd been together, who was to stay how happy they might have been?

"I don't remember them together."

"Well, marriage is more than shared meals," Fannie said. "It's shared everything. And a lifetime is a very long time to go with someone who might feel more like a burden than a blessing."

And as the words came out of her mouth, it occurred to her that she was "preaching to the elders," so to speak. Maybe that was how he had felt when he left town after his *daet* had suggested he marry her.

Jesse turned the horse down a familiar gravel road. This was the road that led to Jesse's house—the one he'd grown up in. They slowed as they came to the drive, and Jesse pulled them to a stop. He turned his attention toward the property.

Another family had moved onto that acreage now. There were some children's sleds leaning up against the woodpile, and a finger of smoke crept up from the chimney. This house had been rented, not owned. So that transition had been a fast one. Menno Hills had a new family in their district now, and the other families with small *kinner* were delighted to have more playmates, and the school would have more students.

"Did you know that if I didn't keep the woodpile waist-high at all times, I'd be in trouble?" Jesse asked softly.

Fannie looked over at him in surprise at the change in topic.

"So you'd always have enough wood, I suppose," she replied. "That way if there was a storm, you wouldn't run out."

"If there was a storm and the wood got depleted to below my waist, I'd still be in trouble," he said, and there was something heavy in tone.

"At all times. There was no excuse. It was my responsibility."

A shiver slid down Fannie's spine. "That seems excessive."

"Sure does," he said, and he sighed. "The bottom half of that woodpile is probably rotten by now. It hasn't been touched since I was old enough to hold an ax."

"Your father had his ways..." she murmured. She wasn't sure what else to say. Caleb used to make her feel uncomfortable when she was younger, but after Jesse had left, Caleb had softened a lot.

"He had his ways," Jesse said bitterly, and he flicked the reins again, and they carried on. "Funny how different a house can look when a new family moves into it. The whole place looks happier now. Downright cheery."

Jesse didn't sound angry now. He sounded sad.

"Jesse, a lot of us had strict parents," Fannie said. The Amish life was a strict one. There were rules to be followed, and they were not allowed to deviate. That was how they maintained their unique way of life. But a strict family was not an unloving family.

"I know," he said.

"They wanted us to learn to do things right. They wanted to keep us from making dangerous mistakes."

"I know."

"They loved us, Jesse! They were our parents. We were their future!"

One of them would be bishop one day. One of them would teach at the schoolhouse, and several of them would serve as deacons and elders. They were most literally the future of Menno Hills, and Fannie's parents had told her and her siblings this fact over and over again. *One day, you'll make the decisions. But not yet. Right now, it's our job to protect you. Learn from us, and when it's your turn, you'll be able to decide.*

"I'm not criticizing your parents," Jesse said, and he turned sad eyes toward her. "Your *mamm* and *daet* were great. My *daet* wasn't."

What had happened between father and son to leave this kind of bitterness after Caleb's death? Was this just his way of grieving?

The road ended with a no-exit sign and a cement barrier to make the message clearer still. But past the sign, there was a large, cleared area where people would park their buggies. And beyond that, the pond stretched out, white and edged with dried cattail reeds. There was no one on the pond tonight, although a skating area had been cleared earlier, and the lines from the blades of the ice skates shone silver in the moonlight.

"Are you really selling Kauffman Books?" she asked.

"Sort of," he said.

"What do you mean, 'sort of'?" she pressed. Was there any halfway when it came to selling a business? There might be. What did she know?

"I'm dismantling it first," Jesse said. "I'm selling the books, the shelves, the furniture... all of that to whomever wants it. And then I'll sell the empty shop to a new investor who wants to put a business there."

"So...you aren't selling the business as a whole?" she asked. "I thought you could do that—sell the whole shop, books and all, to someone who might want to continue running it."

"I don't want to do that."

"Can you make more money doing it separately?" she asked.

"I have no idea." Jesse had that stubborn sound to his voice.

"What if I wanted to buy it—the whole business, I mean."

"Do you have that kind of money?" Jesse shot her a look of surprise.

"I have my inheritance," she said. "It's been in the bank all this time. I need to find something I can invest it in so that I can support myself. Before this, I thought I might get married, but..."

"You've got a farmer interested in marrying you," Jesse said.

"I thought I might fall in love and get married," she amended. "To a man my own age, who isn't currently grieving his dearly loved wife. Besides, I do have my inheritance, and I've been thinking about what kind of business I would like to build for the rest of my life."

"You should open a craft shop," he said.

"I don't want to run a craft shop."

"But yarn always sells. And quilting supplies. You'd always have a business."

"Jesse, you're being impossible!" she said. "You know me—when have I ever been excited about quilting?"

Jesse shot her a grin. "You only need to sell the supplies, Fannie."

"I loved that bookstore." She sobered. "I spent hours in it as a girl. Your *daet* used to let me borrow books when I couldn't afford to buy them, and I'd read them in the back corner of the store. You know that."

"He was nicer to you than he was to me," Jesse muttered.

"I could escape in those books," she went on. "My life might not have been very exciting, but those books let me live a hundred different lives—they let me have adventures I'd never experience on my own. Your *daet* was a good man—"

Jesse cut her off. "My *daet* was not a good man." Fire blazed in his eyes.

Fannie froze. No one spoke about their parents like that here. No one spoke about a deceased parent like that, either! They respected their parents. Loved them. Fannie had lost both of hers in one fateful buggy accident, and she would have given the world to have a few more years with them. Now that they were gone, all she could remember were the sweet memories—baking with her *mamm* on a winter evening, skating with her *daet* and siblings on the pond, talking and laughing around the kitchen table, gardening together and shucking peas in the shade... Even now, after five years, she still got a lump in her throat remembering.

"Your father is dead now," Fannie said quietly. "Whatever frustrations you had with him are done. His time on this earth is over."

"That doesn't change facts," Jesse replied curtly. "And I don't want anything that my father left for me. I'll put together my own life. And that bookshop isn't going to continue."

Fannie didn't answer. Was this how Jesse was grieving? There were stages to grief, and anger was one of them. Perhaps that was the stage he'd landed on now. Maybe he was stuck there—furious with his father for dying. She surveyed him from the corner of her eye.

"I'm sorry," Jesse added, softening his tone. "You should definitely open a business. You're smart, and I think you'd be a success—you can even buy the shop once it's empty. But not Kauffman Books."

He looked very serious about that, but Fannie knew him, too. Jesse wasn't this hard, angry man. At least, he never was in the past.

"What will you do in Indiana?" Fannie asked.

"I'm working as a carpenter. I'll keep doing that. Eventually, I'll open my own shop, once I've built a reputation."

"You could do that here in Menno Hills," she said. "You have a shop…"

"No." Jesse's tone was curt, but he reached over and took her gloved hand in his. He gave her hand a squeeze. "There are things I need to leave behind, Fannie. I'm sorry."

So Jesse was bent on leaving, but there was still a bookshop that had meant the world to Fannie when she'd been growing up. It had meant a great deal to her after Jesse left, too.

Books had filled that lonely hole in her life, and Caleb Kauffman had grown sadder and sadder. He used to welcome her into the shop with a silent nod, and every day that she went by to read, he would ask the same question. *Did you hear from my son?*

Jesse wanted to leave it all behind—leave it in shambles, if he could—but Fannie wasn't going anywhere. And that shop had a heart of its own—even beyond its owner. Maybe she could change Jesse's mind yet.

Because Kauffman Books deserved to live on, to give a little place of refuge to other girls who loved books and stories and ideas... Not every girl had a face that made the boys her age think of commitment. Not every girl had the same options available to her, but there were certain girls with big hearts and inquisitive minds who needed a bookstore like they needed water to drink and air to breathe.

And for the first time since she'd started mulling over her options, Fannie knew exactly what she wanted to do with the rest of her life.

She wanted to run that bookstore.

Chapter Three

Jesse took Fannie out for a burger and fries at Grandma Froese's Family Restaurant. Grandma Froese's had the best burgers in town, with piles of fresh home-cut fries on the side. Jesse dipped his in gravy, and Fannie dipped hers in ketchup, and they shared a complimentary baked apple for dessert. When the Mennonite waitress brought the bill, Fannie reached for it, but Jesse was faster.

"*Nee*," he said. "I'm paying."

"You're doing me a favor, Jesse," she said. "And I'm not expecting you to actually court me, so let me pay my half, at the very least."

"Fannie, I'm a grown man with a full-time job," he said.

"I'm a grown woman shopping for a business," she retorted. "We can argue about who is more able until we're both blue in the face."

Jesse chuckled. "You haven't changed a bit."

She didn't laugh, though.

"Fannie, I'm paying," he said. "Call it my manly pride, but I will not have you paying for dinner when we go out together. Period."

Fannie looked ready to argue again, but then her cheeks pinked. "*Danke.*"

"No problem." He pulled some bills out of his pocket and put the money into the little folder. "Are you ready to head back?"

"*Yah,*" she said. "*Danke* for rescuing me tonight, Jesse. I really do appreciate it."

And for that warm look in her eyes alone, this was worth it.

"Of course, I'll help you out," he said gruffly, not really sure how to respond. "This is what friends are for, isn't it?"

By the time they were heading back toward her home again, the bottles of hot water at their feet were cold, but their bellies were full and it felt good to have a friend at his side. There was another kind of warmth that mattered more.

"I wonder if your farmer will have left by now," Jesse said.

Fannie was quiet, and he glanced over at her. Was his teasing too much? Maybe. But he wasn't sure how else to interact with her. They were cuddled under the thick lap blankets to stay warm, and a man didn't do that with just anyone. He might share a lap blanket with a sister, or a girlfriend…

"My *ankel* says that I can meet Dieter at the Christmas hymn sing tomorrow evening," Fannie said.

"Oh." He chewed the side of his cheek. Moe wasn't going to give up on this introduction so easily, it seemed.

"I'll have to go there with my *aent* and *ankel*, of course," Fannie said, "but you could attend, too, couldn't you?"

His grandparents would be thrilled if he attended, quite honestly. If they thought he was getting involved in the community again, they'd take that as an indication that he might decide to stay. It seemed almost cruel to give them that kind of hope, but it was either that, or they'd want to talk about it whenever he was at home with them.

"*Yah*, I could do that, if you really want the rescuing." He glanced her way again. She was settled against his arm, and he was loathe to move. She felt nice there—smelling faintly of baked apple, and her breath hanging like lace in the air.

"I do want the rescuing," she said. "Just… stick close. Don't give him a chance to talk to me alone. That's all I need. I can handle the rest."

"Sure." And Jesse shouldn't enjoy playing this part as much as he was. He liked being the man she relied on, being her answer to her current problems. It was satisfying, but he couldn't get used to it. At least his time spent in Menno Hills wouldn't be spent on his own jumbled emotions only. He could do some good for Fannie, too. He owed her that much after he'd left so callously last time.

When Jesse dropped her off at home that evening, her *ankel* Moe stood in the doorway and met Jesse's gaze with an even, almost challenging stare.

Fannie hopped out of the buggy, lugging the water bottles with her, and she looked up at Jesse with glittering eyes.

Jesse broke eye contact with the older man and was grateful to turn back to Fannie.

"*Danke*, Jesse," she said quietly, looking up at him from the open buggy door. "I know this isn't comfortable for you, but I really do appreciate it."

"Any time," Jesse said with a lopsided smile. "See you tomorrow at the Christmas hymn sing."

"See you."

He gave her a nod, and watched as she headed around the horse, pausing to pet him, and then up toward the house.

Moe wanted to provide Fannie with a home and a husband—noble, and understandable. But

Jesse was going to make sure Fannie got what she really wanted.

Besides, Fannie didn't need to settle for a man twice her age. What were her aunt and uncle thinking? She didn't need to lower her expectations. Fannie was a quality woman.

As Jesse flicked the reins and pulled the buggy around, he wondered just how annoyed Moe was going to be with him by the end of the hymn sing tomorrow. Because whether or not Jesse wanted to marry Fannie, he had a feeling that Moe had already summed Jesse up, and he had come up wanting.

Just like Jesse had been in his own father's eyes. Never good enough.

The next day, Jesse made up a few signs saying that the bookstore would be open for business for a few days this week, and that everything had to go—books, shelves, everything! And it definitely drew interest. People came through the tightly packed shop buying stacks of books all day—probably the best business day the shop had ever seen—but it didn't seem to make a dent in the stash of books he had to sell. Jesse spent most of the day unpacking boxes of books from the back of the store and bringing them up to the front and ringing up sales.

Several young Amish parents came through,

buying books about nature and farming for their *kinner* for Christmas. Amish Christmas gifts were always simple and useful, and books fell into that category. The Amish folks knew Jesse, and they stopped to talk a little bit, expressing their condolences for his loss, and asking how he was doing.

"*Gut...gut...*" he would say. "As well as can be expected, I suppose."

That was an acceptable answer, it seemed, and it moved people on out of the shop the most quickly.

Jesse knew this work well—he'd done it all of his childhood and adolescence, after all— but there was some satisfaction in knowing that this would be the end of it. He had to get rid of the inventory somehow, and opening the shop for a blowout sale seemed like the easiest way to do it.

Ironically.

Just after noon, Fannie came by during her lunch break. She leaned against the counter as she munched on a sandwich, watching him ring up another sale for an Englisher man who was buying a stack of Anabaptist history books. Her shawl hung loosely around her shoulders, and she hadn't bothered to put on her bonnet, so that her *kapp* shone white and clean. Most of her attention was on the sandwich in her hand, and there was something rather pretty and cheering about her preoccupation with her food.

The history books were clothbound in a sober brown, and he remembered when his *daet* had acquired them. They'd be perfect for the right customer—so his *daet* had claimed. It looked like this man was that customer, because he bought the whole set of six.

Fannie was silent as he worked, and when the man left with his paper bag balanced in his arms, she swallowed a mouthful and said, "Are you making a profit?"

"I'm not trying to make a profit. I'm trying to get rid of books."

"But are you?" she pressed. "I think you should at least try to make as much from these sales as you can. I mean, you don't need to be foolhardy about it. Let this place go with some dignity." *Dignity.* That wasn't the point here. But Fannie must have seen something in his expression, because she quickly added, "For me, if not for yourself. For me..."

"I'm making a bit of a profit," he admitted.

"Doesn't a small part of you enjoy this?" Fannie licked her lips and took another bite of her sandwich. If his *daet* were still alive, he'd have escorted Fannie out until she'd finished her food, he realized bitterly.

But did he enjoy this?

"I like to achieve a goal," he said. "And my goal is to empty this shop."

Fannie nodded, her attention on her food again, and he felt that old stirring of frustration. Because he did like it. He knew where specific books were located—even after having been gone for two years—and he knew what to recommend for someone who wanted something similar.

The bell above the door tinkled and an Englisher woman in a puffy red jacket came inside. She glanced around, her eyes shining.

"Everything's on sale?" she asked.

"Everything."

"Do you have any Amish novels?"

"*Yah.* A whole section. Over here."

He brought her over to the section of shelves and she squatted down to get a better look. Fannie came over and bent down, looking over the woman's shoulder at the Amish fiction.

"I've read all of these," Fannie said. "They're good. Especially this one." She pointed out a novel she'd particularly enjoyed.

"Thanks." The woman smiled up at her and picked up the book to read the back.

Jesse moved toward the front of the store again and Fannie followed. She tucked her wrapper into her cloth lunch bag.

"I have to get back to work," Fannie said. "My lunch break is almost over."

"Right." He glanced out the big window toward Black Bonnet Amish Chocolates across the street. An Englisher wearing a red Santa hat was just going inside. "I guess I'll see you tonight, then."

"You'd better!" Fannie thumped a hand against his chest, and he smiled at the familiar gesture. "Get there early. I'll try to drag my feet and arrive a bit later, if I can. But be there when I arrive, okay?"

"*Yah*, I can do that."

Fannie pulled her shawl closer around her shoulders and headed for the door. The bell tinkled again at her leaving, and he watched her out the window as she jogged across the street, narrowly missing being splashed by a passing van going through a slushy puddle.

Jesse hadn't been looking forward to this Christmas hymn sing. There would be plenty of reminders of how he was supposed to forgive. There would be a lot of familiar faces wanting some sort of explanation for missing his own father's funeral. But somehow, Fannie's gratitude made him look forward to it just a little bit. He did like having a goal. Today, he had a goal of selling as many books as he possibly could, and tonight his goal was to intercept Fannie's farmer as many times as possible.

Goals made even painful things feel like successes. And today, it seemed, was all about the goals.

As Jesse anticipated, his grandparents were delighted that he'd be attending the Christmas hymn sing. His *dawdie* had a cough, though, and his *mammi* liked to go to bed much earlier than the young people did, and they'd decided to stay in with the warm stove and each other for company.

"But I'm glad you'll go, Jesse," Mammi said, putting a gentle hand on his arm. "It's good for you *youngie* to get out and be sociable. You need a reason to be happy again, dear boy. Your *daet* would have wanted that."

Somehow, Jesse doubted that his *daet* would have wanted him to be off helping his best pal dodge an arranged marriage. He would have been sour about that. He would have called it meddling in business not his own. And as for finding reason to smile again, Jesse's *daet* had never bothered much about that while he was alive.

Mammi headed to the sink to start on some dishes, and she started humming a familiar old tune. *Stille Nacht.* "Silent Night."

A long time ago, when Jesse was a boy and Fannie had been his dearest friend, he used to listen to the adults singing *Stille Nacht* at the hymn sings at various gatherings. It had been soothing, and listening to the song about the quiet night when Jesus had been born used to fill his heart with hope.

Jesus had come to this world in the middle of farmyard animals in a stable. And Jesse couldn't think of a better place for a baby to arrive. At least in his childish view of the world. But now, that old song plucked at a different string in his heart.

Where had Gott been when Jesse was a little boy in need of love after his *mamm* had died and his sisters had moved away? Where had Gott been when Jesse had been starved for some encouragement and some kind word from his father? And where had he been when his father would look at that woodpile, deem it not tall enough, and take the leather strap out of the drawer?

Where had Gott been then? Because Jesse had felt utterly alone. Sometimes, silence wasn't peaceful. Some silent nights were desperately, desperately lonely.

The Christmas hymn sing was held at the Hochstetler farm, and when Fannie arrived with her aunt and uncle, the house was already lit up with kerosene lamps, and the sound of happy chatting and cheerful voices filtered out into the winter night. Fannie sat in the back of the buggy, a plate piled high with sugar cookies balanced on her lap. She'd made them herself— Aent Bethany had insisted, not that Fannie ever minded doing the baking. She enjoyed it. But she knew why it mattered tonight. Her cookies would be presented to Dieter Glick as proof that she was competent in the kitchen.

A neat line of buggies was parked by the stable, and Ankel Moe unhitched the horse and led him toward the corral next to the stable where other horses stood together, blankets over their backs to keep them warm in the winter night.

"Aent Bethany?" Fannie plucked the edge of her *aent*'s thick shawl, holding the plate of cookies against her hip as they headed toward the house together.

"*Yah*, Fannie?"

"Does it matter at all that I don't want to meet Dieter?"

A brisk wind swirled around Fannie's skirt, and she tugged her shawl closer around herself.

"What are you afraid of?" her aunt asked quietly.

"I'm not scared. I just don't want to."

"What if he's wonderful?" Aent Bethany

asked. "What if he's handsome and kind and gentle, and you decide you like him?"

"He's almost forty."

"You don't know how his age sits on him, though," Aent Bethany said. "Your *ankel* is older than I am. Don't you want to get married and have a family of your own?"

"What if I don't?" she countered.

Aent Bethany met Fannie's gaze. "Really?"

Fannie's heart started to beat a little faster at the lie on the tip of her tongue. But she wouldn't tell an untruth. She might fight for her freedom, but she wouldn't use lies in her arsenal.

"I do want to be married one day," Fannie said. "But I want to fall in love, like my *mamm* did. I don't want an arrangement. And until I fall in love, I want to find a way to support myself."

"Supporting yourself financially is harder than you might think," her *aent* replied. "I did just that for two years before I met your *ankel*. It's difficult. It takes more money than you think, and it takes more work than you think to make that money. It's tiring—every day is utterly exhausting. It's not a life of carefree freedom."

"But it would give me time," Fannie said earnestly. "And my *mamm* said she knew the moment she met my *daet* that she wanted to marry him."

"Well, you haven't even met Dieter yet, so I don't think that's a fair comparison." Aent Bethany looked in the direction of the corral where Ankel Moe was getting the horse settled, then back at Fannie. "Fannie, I don't want to push you into a relationship you don't want. But I'm going to tell you something that might change your mind about things."

"Oh?"

"Your *ankel*'s health is not as strong as it used to be," Aent Bethany said, lowering her voice to a whisper. "He would hate it if he knew I'd told you, but he's been getting more of those chest pains, and he needs rest. That's why we need to go to Florida and retire. I wish we had more time, but I'm afraid that we don't. We need to do something for you, and we don't have a lot of time. And then as if it were Gott's own will, Dieter came looking for a wife."

Fannie's breath caught in her throat.

"How sick is Ankel Moe?" she asked.

"He'll be all right with a doctor's care and proper rest, but we can't go on with this farm—that's just the truth of it. So let us help you get a home of your own first, before we have to leave. Please, Fannie."

Fannie's aunt and uncle were doing their best, and she could see why they needed to leave Menno Hills. Sometimes time did run out.

The side door opened, and two of Fannie's cousins appeared in the window. They'd grown up together, gone to school together, celebrated birthdays together, too. Now both were married with babies in their arms, and they brightened when they saw Fannie and waved.

But it wasn't a cousin standing in the doorway. It was Jesse. He'd taken off his hat—it would be in a pile with all the other men's hats—and his hair was a little bit mussed. He wore a clean white shirt that betrayed some of those carpentry muscles he'd gained over the last two years. The cold didn't seem to bother him. He gave her aunt a broad smile.

"Good evening, Aent Bethany," he said. He'd always called her that, because Fannie had. "It's good to see you."

"Jesse," Aent Bethany said, looking a little confused at the sudden and direct attention. "How are you?"

"I'm doing all right, considering." His smile dimmed. "How are you doing?"

He stepped back as Fannie and Aent Bethany came inside. There was a pile of men's coats on a folding table, and another table covered with men's hats and women's black bonnets. Women's shawls were hung one on top of the other on pegs on the wall, and all of the items looked identical to an untrained eye. But everyone had a little mark or even their initials somewhere on their items of clothing so they would know them again. And sometimes they'd get mixed up, which only gave people reason to visit each other and swap a bonnet or a shawl.

"Hi," Jesse said softly, his voice pitched for her ears alone.

"Hi," she whispered back.

"I was waiting for you," he said.

The kitchen and sitting room normally had a wall between them, but it was collapsable, so that now the two rooms were one large room, with pies and baked goods waiting on the kitchen table that was pushed aside, and Jesse turned that charming smile of his onto her, and she had to forcibly remind herself that he was only playing a part.

"For how long?" Fannie asked.

"I've been here for half an hour already. I've eaten almost a whole pie."

That was the Jesse she knew, and she burst out laughing. She handed her plate of sugar cookies to Jesse to hold for her while she took off her boots then, and put her bonnet and shawl with the women's things, as did her aunt.

"You better have saved me a piece, Jesse," she said.

"Did you make these?" Jesse asked, looking down at the cookies with interest.

"Of course."

Some younger girls were looking through the hymnal for their favorite Christmas carols, and they started singing "Oh Come, All Ye Faithful" together. The men were visiting on the far side of the potbellied woodstove, all of them in sock feet. There was one man there that Fannie didn't immediately recognize, and she could guess at his identity. He was tall, broad shouldered, and he had a dark, full beard. He also had just a little bit of a belly—he looked married. Or maybe he just looked older. She tried not to be seen inspecting him, and when one of the other men looked up, she dropped her gaze.

Five *kinner* sat near the food, a little separated from the other *kinner*, looking shy. The oldest boy looked about twelve, and the oldest girl was probably ten. There were two more younger boys and a toddler girl.

"Is that him?" Fannie whispered.

"*Yah*. I already introduced myself," Jesse said.

"You did?"

"Of course. Am I supposed to run away from the man?"

"*Nee*, but—" Fannie looked around Jesse's shoulder, and Dieter was deep in conversation with some other men. Jesse didn't seem the least bit intimidated, and maybe that was a good thing.

Jesse peeled the plastic wrap off the plate of sugar cookies and he headed over to the shy *kinner* and held them out. The oldest boy and girl sat on one kitchen chair that was pushed up against the wall, and one little boy who looked to be about four leaned against his brother's knee, and another boy who looked about six or seven was eyeing the plate of cookies with interest.

"Would you like some cookies?" Jesse asked.

Five pairs of stunned eyes looked up at him.

"They're very good." Jesse picked one up and took a bite. "My friend made them, and her cookies are the best in Menno Hills."

Fannie pretended she didn't notice the compliment, but she warmed at it all the same. The *kinner* accepted a cookie each and started to eat them in a spray of crumbs. Then Jesse held the plate out to Fannie.

"Want one?" he asked with a teasing little smile.

"I should test them to see if they're as good as you claim," she said with a low laugh. Then she turned to the children. "There are some other *kinner* upstairs, you know. I know they'd like to play with you."

The little girls looked up at the boys questioningly. The other children who'd been in the kitchen were thundering on up the staircase.

"Go try, and if they aren't nice to you, I'll stomp up there to tell them they have to," Jesse said with a wink. The oldest boy laughed at that—he knew Jesse was only joking.

"Come on, let's go up and see what they're doing," he said, and the five *kinner* made their way up the back staircase, the littlest girl in the oldest girl's arms, toward the bedrooms where Fannie could hear laughter filtering down.

Fannie watched them go—trailing along together in a sad little group. They were very young to be facing life without their *mamm*, and to be looking forward to another woman to take her place in their home.

"They look like good *kinner*," Fannie said softly.

"*Yah*, they do. Tempted yet?"

Jesse met her gaze seriously.

"No." She pitied the *kinner*, that was true. She knew what it felt like to lose a parent. She'd lost both of hers at once. She knew what it was to miss a mother. But she couldn't be theirs, and she knew that in the depths of her heart.

"Just checking," Jesse murmured, and his gaze flickered toward the men. Ankel Moe had come inside, and he and Dieter were talking together. Then both men looked in their direction. "Because I have a feeling you're about to officially meet Menno Hills' most eligible widower."

Ankel Moe and Dieter were walking slowly in their direction, their gazes cast down as they talked together. This was it, and all of her instincts told her to get out of this room—outside in the cold, upstairs with the *kinner*—anywhere but here!

"Just stay with me," she breathed, and when she looked over at Jesse, she found his blue gaze lingering on her face.

"Of course," he said. "I'm not going anywhere."

And she instantly felt better. Good old Jesse. He always had been the best of friends.

Chapter Four

Jesse liked Dieter, and he really wished this widowed farmer was less likeable. Dieter had a firm handshake and a direct look—two things a man was forced to respect. He'd also been very gentle with his *kinner* before Fannie had arrived. Jesse had watched him lick his finger and clean some jam off the toddler's cheek, and even now as Dieter and Moe walked up, he could see Dieter looking around for them.

"They went upstairs to play with the other *kinner*," Jesse said, and he stuck out his hand first. As if to confirm Jesse's words, there was a peal of children's laughter from overhead, and the toddler appeared on the stairs. Her older sister gathered her up in her arms and carried her back upstairs.

Dieter's expression softened. "*Danke.* I was wondering where they went. Jesse, right?"

They shook hands once more—already having shaken hands when they met earlier—and Moe cast Jesse a mildly annoyed look.

"Jesse Kauffman," he replied. "That's right."

"This is my niece, Fannie," Moe said.

Dieter turned his smile toward Fannie, and Jesse felt an immediate, unwelcome pang of jealousy. Fannie didn't want Dieter—nice as he might be—and that was what this was about.

Fannie gave Dieter a wordless nod.

"Fannie, this is Dieter Glick," Moe said. "I'm sure I mentioned him. He's visiting for Christmas. Did you see his *kinner*?"

"*Yah*," Fannie said. "You have beautiful *kinner*."

"*Danke*." Dieter brightened. "They are good *kinner*, too. They mind me well, and they have good hearts."

"They were very polite," Jesse cut in with a smile. "I gave them cookies to eat. I hope you don't mind."

"Of course not," Dieter said, but he didn't turn from Fannie. "Fannie, I heard that you lost your parents a few years ago. I'm very sorry to hear it. That's not easy."

"No, it isn't," Fannie said.

"My *kinner* know the pain of losing a mother, too," Dieter said. "They are so young to know that heartache. I'm hoping to find a new mother for them. They desperately need a loving *mamm* to take care of them."

"I'm sorry for your loss, Dieter," Fannie said quietly.

Moe angled his head at Jesse, silently beckoning him to come away. Jesse understood exactly what Moe wanted, but when he looked down at Fannie, he noticed that her hands folded in front of her were clasped in a white-knuckle grip. He looked up at Moe again, and Moe angled his head again with a serious look on his face. An older man was telling him to let them talk, and he had a choice ahead of him—cooperate with Moe, or stand by his word to Fannie.

"Dieter," Jesse said, injecting himself into the conversation. "I hear you farm?"

"*Yah.*" Dieter was forced to look over at him now. "Alfalfa and potatoes. I know it sounds like a strange mix, but both sell well out there, and I'm able to keep on top of it with some hired help come potato season."

"I'm curious about potatoes," Jesse said. "Do you harvest all those plants by hand?"

"*Yah.* It takes time, but I've got a good variety that produces very well. I have enough for my own family for the year, plus I sell to the local grocery stores, and I put a sign up at the front of my drive. That brings in quite a few customers."

"I found that mine aren't doing terribly well,"

Jesse said. "Last year about half of mine rotted. Do you have any advice?"

Fannie murmured something Jesse couldn't make out, and she slipped away. Moe rubbed a hand over his forehead and just looked defeated. But Jesse had promised Fannie that he'd intercept her uncle's mission to make a match, and he was determined to see it through.

Jesse chatted with Dieter for a few more minutes. Dieter had some advice about how to grow good potatoes, which was very helpful. And then the Christmas singing started with some women in the corner singing "Angels We Have Heard on High," and when Jesse looked up, he saw that Fannie was standing on the edge of the group, and he could make out her voice.

She had a pretty singing voice—she always had—and for just a moment, he caught himself listening for just her voice in the choir. He realized that Dieter was standing next to him, looking in the same direction he was. Jesse sighed. At least he'd gotten Fannie away from Dieter. He couldn't help it if the man could see her across a room.

The men joined in with the Gloria chorus, and for the next few minutes, the whole house shook with the reverberation of joyful Christmas carols. The *kinner* came down the stairs, small feet thundering as they hurried to join in the music. Everyone loved singing carols.

Dieter's *kinner* pressed around him, and Jesse slipped off to the side. The music was comforting to him, too. This had been a tough last few weeks with his father's death, and somehow the songs about Jesus being born were touching a soft part of his heart tonight.

When the men circled around a song book to choose the next carol, he felt a soft tug on his sleeve, and Fannie slipped past him. He turned and followed her, heading away from the crowd of neighbors and into the kitchen. Some women were by the table, arranging another plate of squares and cookies, so Jesse and Fannie headed over to the staircase and stopped there.

"*Danke*," Fannie breathed.

"He seems like a nice man, for what it's worth," Jesse said quietly.

"He could be my *daet*!"

"*Yah*." Jesse shot her a rueful smile. "I know. I get it. He's much older than us, but he's a nice man, all the same. He seems like a good *daet*, too."

And Jesse had a soft spot for good fathers. He hadn't had a kind or gentle father of his own. Dieter's *kinner* had come back downstairs and were standing close to him, and Dieter had

"Good."

Another Christmas carol started up, and Jesse's stomach rumbled. He nodded toward the table of desserts.

"Do you want to get something else to eat?" he asked.

Fannie shook her head. "*Nee*, I'm okay. You go ahead."

When he looked down at Fannie, he saw her gaze trained on the back of Dieter and his *kinner*. She looked nervous, and she chewed her bottom lip.

"Fannie," he said. "You don't have to marry him."

"I know." She shook the uncertainty off her face. "It's just that my *ankel* is more sick than I realized. He's been getting chest pains. My *aent* is worried."

"And you think you need to marry Dieter to set them free?" he asked with a frown.

"*Nee*. I think I need to get a place of my own and a job that will support me so I can set them free," she replied. "But they need to go to Florida."

"I'm getting you cookies," he said gruffly, and he headed over to the table and picked up a plate. Fannie might not feel like eating, but with something tasty in front of her, she might picked up the toddler in his arms, and the two little boys leaned against him on either side, the older *kinner* sandwiching them in. Those *kinner* weren't afraid of their *daet*. Jesse never would have dared to touch his father in public, and if he felt his father's hand on his shoulder, he knew he was in trouble and was going to get a whooping once they were home.

"Was I rude?" she asked, her voice low.

"Not at all. You were perfectly polite. You can't marry a man just to avoid social awkwardness."

"Tell my *ankel* that," she chuckled, and she flashed him a quick smile. "*Danke* for the distraction. You were wonderful."

"Any time," he murmured back

His pulse sped up at that smile. Dieter had noticed something he liked in Fannie—Jesse could see that plainly. And he couldn't blame the man. When Fannie gave him a grin like that, it made his own pulse speed up, too. But he'd already nearly ruined their friendship once and he wasn't about to risk that again by flirting with her now.

"Now, if we can just keep you around long enough for Dieter to find someone else marry, I'll be fine," she said softly.

"I'll be around," Jesse said. Even couldn't lever him away.

change her mind. It was some little thing he could do to help.

Or he could let her buy the shop...

He brushed that thought aside. *Nee*, he couldn't do that. The very thought of Kauffman Books carrying on after his *daet*'s death made his own chest constrict. That shop with all of its dusky memories needed to be dismantled. His *daet*'s reign of terror was over, and Jesse would not allow a shred of what his *daet* had built to remain standing.

Mammi and Dawdie thought that business was a gift, but it wasn't. It was a pair of shackles meant to keep Daet's influence over him, even after his death.

And Jesse piled a plate with cookies, matrimonial cake and some handmade chocolates.

Maybe he needed a bit of comfort tonight, too.

When the evening wound down, Dieter went out to hitch up his buggy first, and then he came back for his family. The *kinner* were tired—the toddler draped asleep over one of Dieter's shoulders, and his oldest boy carrying the youngest boy in his arms. The next youngest's eyes were only half-open. They'd all fall asleep in the buggy ride back to wherever they were staying.

Buggy blankets were warming in a nice pile by the woodstove, and Bethany picked out Dieter's blankets and handed them to Moe. They'd be tucked around the *kinner* in the buggy to keep them warm on their way back.

"It was nice to meet you, Fannie," Dieter said.

"Good night," she said. "It was nice to meet you, as well."

Politeness, right? That was all that was?

Dieter and the *kinner* headed out together, and Jesse stood in the kitchen with Bethany, Moe and Fannie. Fannie looked tired suddenly, her face paler than usual, and Jesse could feel that his guard duty was now over.

"We should head home, too," Bethany said quietly. "How are you feeling, Moe?"

"Me?" Moe rubbed the heel of his hand over the side of his chest. "I'm fine. But if you're tired, we should head home, I suppose."

"*Yah*, I'm tired," Bethany said, but there was worry in her gaze.

What had Fannie said about her *ankel*'s health? Moe wasn't the same gruff, strong, older man who Jesse remembered. He'd aged more than Jesse had realized over the last two years. And while he knew that Moe was annoyed with him for having gotten in the way of his introductions between Dieter and Fannie, Jesse couldn't very well let Moe go out there and hitch up without giving him a hand, knowing what he now knew.

"Let me help you hitch up," Jesse said quickly. "I need to get home, as well."

Bethany cast him a grateful look, and so did Fannie.

Jesse and Moe both got their coats and boots on, and they headed outside into the dark winter night. Moe didn't say anything as they went to the corral and called their horses. Jesse left his horse tied to the fence by the gate, and they led Moe's horse back to the Flaud buggy.

"Can I say something to you, man-to-man?" Moe asked, his voice low.

Here it was—he was about to be told off for ruining Fannie's chances.

Jesse swallowed. "Of course."

He wasn't sure he wanted to hear this, but he couldn't very well run away from it.

Moe backed his horse between the traces, then met Jesse's gaze.

"My niece has been through enough rejection in the last two years," Moe said quietly. "She's a wonderful girl—kind, smart, talented. She deserves a good marriage to a man who will adore her."

"I agree," Jesse replied.

"I am trying to introduce my niece to a man who will value her," Moe said.

"He's almost twice her age," Jesse countered.

"Are you going to marry her?" Moe demanded. "Or are you going to enjoy her company and then leave like you did last time?"

Jesse opened his mouth to answer, and then clamped it shut. He wasn't about to lie to Moe. Fannie wouldn't want that, either. This was supposed to be a harmless ploy to give her space, nothing more.

Moe nodded slowly as if he understood. "When you left last time, Fannie was crushed."

That sounded like an exaggeration, though.

"I know she was angry," Jesse said.

"I stand by my words, Jesse. She was crushed. She lost weight. She lost the color in her face. She lost the sparkle in her eye, and every single day she walked to the mailbox, and I'd watch her check the box, and she'd visibly deflate when there was no letter from you. She did that for almost six months before she finally accepted that you weren't going to write."

Jesse stood there, frozen. Had he really hurt Fannie that badly? He hadn't known that! If he'd known she'd missed him that much, he would have written. Because he'd longed to write, but he couldn't face her questions and demands for honesty! He'd been so angry at his *daet*, so ready for some freedom, so filled with his own bitterness, and he'd known what Fannie would demand of him—forgiveness. She'd insist that he be the bigger man, and he couldn't do it.

"It was an uphill climb after that," Moe went on. "She slowly got happier. She put you behind her. I know that trying to arrange a marriage between the two of you was a mistake—I'll apologize for that, Jesse. I'm sorry. I was wrong. You two were good friends and nothing more. But you walked out on her as her friend, too, and it broke something inside of her. I was wrong to try and suggest a marriage between the two of you, but you were wrong for treating her like she was disposable. That was on you, Jesse."

"I didn't know," Jesse said. "I had no idea."

That image of Fannie crushed—it was heartbreaking. He couldn't imagine Fannie letting anything reduce her like that. The Fannie he knew bossed him around and refused to be set up with a widower pushing forty. That was the Fannie he knew.

"Well, she's happy now. And she's strong again, and there's a good man who wants to marry her," Moe said. "And if you are her friend again, you won't try to stand in the way of it."

"Moe, she's not interested!" Jesse said.

"She hasn't even talked to him," Moe said. "Not really. And I get it. She's scared of getting her hopes up and having them dashed. She's afraid of another man walking out on her. She's got a more tender heart than you know, Jesse.

She's not just a buddy or a pal. She's a young *woman*."

Moe was right, of course. Fannie wasn't just a pal. She had more depth to her than any other woman he'd ever met.

"I won't go breaking her heart, Moe," Jesse said. "I promise you that."

It wasn't possible this time around. She'd only asked for his help in putting off a marriage arrangement. She had her plans, and he had his. This time around, they weren't letting any outside meddling affect their close friendship.

"See that you don't," Moe said, bending to hitch up his horse.

Jesse started doing up the buckles on the other side, but Moe's description of Fannie's heartbreak had seared itself into his mind.

It was a good warning. He'd hurt her more than he'd ever realized, and he'd best be careful not to do that again.

Ankel Moe was already out working the farm and Aent Bethany was up earlier than expected and was already dressed and working on breakfast when Fannie came downstairs.

"I can help with that," Fannie said, and she took over chopping potatoes.

"*Danke*, Fannie."

Her aunt headed over to the stove and bent

down to stoke up the fire a little higher in the firebox. Her aunt seemed quiet this morning, and less cheery.

"It looks like it will be a sunny day out," Fannie said. "The sky is clear."

Her aunt nodded, and Fannie sighed.

"Are you angry with me?" Fannie asked.

"I'm disappointed, Fannie. You were rude yesterday."

"I wasn't! I said hello and I chatted with Dieter a little bit."

"You sent Jesse after him to keep him away from you," Aent Bethany said. "That was clear as a sunny day."

Fannie's face warmed at the quiet reprimand.

"What if I did?" Fannie asked. "I won't lie. But I much prefer Jesse to Dieter."

"What if you're wrong?" Aent Bethany asked. "Have you thought of that? What if Jesse ends up being just the same old Jesse—handsome, sweet, complicated, and headed out of town without you?"

Her aunt knew her better than she liked to admit, and she knew Jesse rather well, too. But Jesse hadn't changed all that much, and Fannie couldn't argue with that, so she didn't say anything.

"And what if you end up regretting being so cold to Dieter?" Aent Bethany went on. "What if I was right, in all my old-lady wisdom that seems so ridiculous to you right now? What if Dieter ends up being a truly decent man with a good heart, and you miss your chance at a happy and settled life because you preferred a man who already proved himself to be unreliable?"

Fannie felt her chin tremble—the rising tears being part shame and part frustration. Did no one care if she simply did not want to marry the man? Shouldn't her personal feelings factor in here somewhere? The truth was, she wasn't going to marry Jesse or Dieter! She was going to find a way to support herself.

Fannie helped her aunt make breakfast, and when her uncle came in from chores, they all sat down together to eat. The food felt like sawdust in her mouth, though.

Jesse's buggy pulled up when they had just cleared the table, and Fannie looked outside to see Jesse in profile. He was a handsome man, but it wasn't his good looks that softened her whenever she looked at him. She knew him better than anyone—at least, she had two years ago. And he was a gentle, good man. Sure, he was complicated, but he deserved someone who understood him, too.

"Is Esther Mae here?" Aent Bethany asked, looking toward the window. Normally, Esther Mae was the one who picked her up for work.

"Jesse is driving me," Fannie said.

Her aunt nodded grimly. "All right."

Fannie expected more of a comment from her aunt, but when she didn't get it, she picked up her thermos of soup and her bagged sandwich and headed out the side door. She pulled the door solidly shut behind her and headed over to Jesse's buggy. He gave her a hesitant smile as she hoisted herself up onto the seat next to him.

"Everything okay this morning?" he asked.

"Fine." She leaned back into the seat and pulled the lap blanket over her legs. "Good morning, by the way."

"Good morning," he said, and he flicked the reins. The horse started forward and they turned around in a tight circle, heading back up the drive.

Jesse kept his eyes on the road, both hands on the reins, and Fannie could feel the space between them like the air from a freezer.

"How are you?" she asked.

"Fine." His gaze flickered in her direction, but whatever friendly balance they'd had last night seemed to be gone.

"Not you, too," she said.

"What?" Jesse asked.

"I have my *ankel* and *aent* both upset with me because I won't consider Dieter Glick, and now you're acting strange, too."

"Your *ankel* gave me a good talking-to last night," he said.

"What did he say?" she asked, and her stomach fluttered in worry.

"He said that—" Jesse leaned forward to check both ways before he guided the horse onto the road. "He said that when I left the first time, I really crushed you."

"Oh. That." Fannie looked out the window, her mind whirling.

"*Yah*, that," Jesse said. "I didn't know I had upset you that badly, Fannie. I was so wrapped up in my own anger and bitterness toward my *daet* that all I could think about was getting away and starting fresh somewhere else."

"It's fine," she said hurriedly.

"Moe said you kept checking the mail," he said.

Did her uncle have to tell all of her secrets? But then, Ankel Moe was assuming something that wasn't actually happening.

"And he thinks that you're taking me out romantically," she said. "Right... I can see why he's telling you that now."

"He doesn't want me to break your heart," Jesse said.

It was embarrassing having her heartbreak so public and obvious. If she'd been able to hide it better, she would have, but she would not admit to Jesse how deeply he'd hurt her. She was wiser now.

"Well, no worry there, right?" she asked, trying to sound brighter than she felt. "We're friends. We were friends before you left, and we're friends now. We can't let the older generation drive us apart just because they see romance and marriage behind every tree, Jesse."

Jesse's expression didn't relax, though, and his jaw stayed tense.

"I didn't mean to hurt you like that," Jesse said, his voice low. "I'm sorry."

Fannie had had to look long and hard at her reliance on her friendship with Jesse in the months after he had left. But she'd learned to stand up on her own two feet, and to rely on Gott, not a man. That had been a painful but necessary lesson in her estimation.

"It's okay, Jesse. I'm fine." She leaned over and nudged his arm, and he looked down at her. She gave him a smile. "I'm fine."

"*Yah.*" A smile touched his lips, too. "Okay. I'm glad."

They drove along the snowy road, sunlight glittering off the untrampled snow in the fields beside them. Loose hay and hoof prints surrounded a feeder with a round bale of hay, the cattle milling around close together for warmth.

"Don't let my *ankel* make you feel bad, Jesse," she said. "I appreciate you helping me."

"He's worried about you," Jesse said.

"Everyone is worried about a single woman," she replied with a low laugh. "He'll stop worrying when I can get a job that will pay enough to keep me. Then he'll know I'm provided for."

"*Nee*, I mean, he's worried about more than that," Jesse said. "He's worried that you're afraid of being rejected. He blames himself for pushing us together. And he blames me for leaving like I did. But he really does fear that you're going to be too cautious now and miss out on opportunities to get married because of it."

Fannie sighed. She couldn't maintain the smile, so she let it go. Everyone was worrying about her a little too much. Perhaps they should worry more about pushing her into a relationship she had no interest in pursuing. There was life outside of wedlock—she'd seen it with Esther Mae and with Iris Bischel. Women could live happy and fulfilled lives without a husband. They did it all the time.

"Maybe I am cautious," she admitted. "But there is good reason for it."

"Because of me?" Jesse asked.

"Not completely," she replied. "*Yah*, it hurt me a great deal when you left the way you did. Especially after they suggested me as a wife for you, and you ran out of town so fast we could almost see the dust trail behind you."

"It wasn't about you!" Jesse turned toward her. "You have to believe me."

Wasn't it, though? He certainly hadn't wanted to marry her, and if Fannie had to be completely honest, if Jesse had asked her, she would have said yes. She'd been halfway in love with her best friend, and it wouldn't have taken much to convince her to give him her whole heart. But he'd never seen her that way, and she'd thought she'd been fine with it, right up until Ankel Moe and Caleb Kauffman put their heads together.

"Whether your quick exit was because of me or not, I'd leaned on you too much," Fannie replied. "I thought I could count on you being my friend for the rest of my life, but that was naive of me."

"I am your friend." Jesse caught her gaze and held it. "I am."

"I'm glad you're back," she said. "I really am. And I wish you'd stay, but I know you won't. But that's okay. Jesse, I made my peace with all of this. I'm sorry that Ankel Moe is worried, but you don't have to worry about me, too, okay?"

"Okay." He turned his attention back to the road. "I'm glad. Because I have a favor to ask of you."

"What's that?" she asked.

"I want to go to the graveyard," he said. "I want see where they buried Daet."

Fannie could see how hard that was for Jesse to even say, and she put a gloved hand on his coat sleeve.

"Would you—" He cleared his throat. "Would you come with me?"

And how could she say no? This was Jesse, the friend who had filled her heart for years, and she knew his weaknesses. He'd never dealt with strong emotion very well, and it was no surprise that his father's death was so difficult for him to deal with. They may have had troubles in their father-son relationship, but Caleb had still been his *daet*.

"Of course, I'll come," she said. "When do you want to go?"

"How about after work?" he asked. "I'll bring you a burger to go from Grandma Froese's for supper, and we could pass by on the way home."

Jesse needed to see the spot in the community graveyard where his *daet* lay, and she was honored that he'd chosen her to go along with him. He could have asked his *mammi* or *dawdie*—they would have gladly gone along—but he hadn't. He'd wanted her, and that warmed a place in her heart that had always been reserved only for him.

"I'd be happy to," she said.

***

When Fannie arrived at the Black Bonnet Amish Chocolates shop that morning, she went straight to the woodstove to warm up. Wide windows let in ample light, and when the mornings were dim like today, they lit kerosene lamps on the walls, which gave a cheery glow. They had propane-powered refrigerators and freezers in the back to keep the chocolates fresh before they put them in the display case, and Esther Mae was using a pair of metal tongs to set out an arrangement of Lamb Ears, which were chocolate-dipped potato chips. They were a new creation made by Miriam Yoder, Esther Mae's niece by marriage, and they'd been selling very well.

"*Guder mariye*," Fannie said, shutting the door behind her.

"Good morning, Fannie," Esther Mae said with a smile. "It's nice to see you."

"*Guder mariye*," Iris echoed, coming out of the kitchen with a platter of chocolate truffles held in front of her.

"We didn't see you at the hymn sing, Esther Mae," Fannie said. "Iris and I were both there."

"Oh, I was having a quiet evening in by myself," Esther Mae replied. "Was it a good time?"

"A very good time," Iris agreed. She cast Fannie a smile.

Iris was tall and slim, in her late thirties, and with a practiced hand at making Esther Mae's chocolate recipes.

"You seemed to have a good time with Jesse Kauffman, *yah*?" Iris asked with an impish little smile.

"Jesse and I have been friends for ages," Fannie said. "I'm glad he's back for a little while."

"He's not staying?" Esther Mae asked.

"*Nee*, he's got a job waiting on him. He's just here until after Christmas," Fannie replied. She thought she'd managed to sound confident in that, even though she dearly wished Jesse would stay longer.

"One of my old school friends is visiting over Christmas, too," Iris said. "I think you met him, Fannie. Dieter Glick."

Fannie looked up in surprise. "You know him?"

"*Yah*. I went to school with him and his sisters in Indiana," Iris replied. "It's nice to see him with the *kinner*. I hadn't seen him since his wedding."

"Did you attend?" Esther Mae asked.

"*Yah*, I did. Sadie was such a kind woman. They were very much in love. It was a wonderful wedding." Iris put the tray of chocolates on top of the display case, and Esther Mae picked it up, and began to arrange the next section of chocolate truffles.

"So you must know him a little bit, at least," Esther Mae said.

"He's a good man," Iris said. "He adored his wife. She passed away about six months ago."

"So he's grieving," Fannie said. Both women looked over at her then, and Fannie felt her face warm. "I mean—six months isn't long."

"I imagine it's a long enough time with five *kinner* and a job to keep," Esther Mae said.

"Rumor has it that Dieter has been looking your direction, Fannie," Iris said quietly.

Rumor was right this time around. Were her coworkers going to nudge her toward Dieter, too?

"I'm much younger than he is," Fannie said.

"Plenty of younger woman have found quality husbands in older men," Esther Mae said. "There is something to be said for some maturity."

Fannie tried to put a cap on her rising irritation, but it was difficult. After her aunt's pointed words and her uncle telling Jesse far too much, she just wanted a day of selling chocolate without someone pressuring her about a wedding! Fannie didn't answer, and she went into the back room and took off her shawl and stepped out of her boots. She had a pair of work shoes she had left on the shoe rack, and she slipped them on. When she emerged into the shop again, Esther Mae and Iris both cast her apologetic looks.

"We don't mean to meddle," Iris said. "He's just a very nice man. I should tell you that. He's very kind, he's a good *daet* and when I knew him, he was very decent."

"Maybe you should get to know him better, Iris," Fannie suggested. That would solve her problem nicely!

"He's not looking my way, is he?" Iris asked with a low laugh. "It's a mistake to go after a man who isn't looking in my direction. I'd live to regret that."

And Fannie looked out the window just then to see Jesse outside shoveling snow off the walk in front of his shop. His attention was on the work in front of him.

Jesse had left town at the mere suggestion that he marry Fannie, and whatever her feelings for him, he'd not returned them. There was wisdom in Iris's words—letting herself feel romantically toward a man who wasn't looking in her direction was a painful mistake, and Fannie wasn't going to make that particular mistake again, either.

"All I want to do is enjoy my Christmas," Fannie said. "And I'm also looking for a second job, if either of you hear of anything."

"Another job?" Esther Mae asked.

"I need to make more money if I'm going to provide for myself eventually, like you do," Fannie said. "And I won't be pushed into a marriage I don't want just to feed myself."

Esther Mae nodded slowly. "No one would ask that of you. It's wise to think about your own future, though."

Her uncle and aunt might ask that of her, but Fannie didn't want to say that. Maybe her uncle and aunt had her best interest at heart, and it wasn't out of malice or cruelty, but they certainly did want her to consider a marriage with Dieter Glick. And while Dieter might be a very kind man, Fannie couldn't even imagine herself as his wife. The very thought put a shiver down her spine.

"So you'll keep an eye out?" Fannie asked hopefully.

"I'll let you know if I hear of any openings," Esther Mae replied.

And that would have to do. The clock on the wall clicked over to nine, and Fannie flipped the sign on the window to Open. It was time to start their day.

Chapter Five

Jesse sat in the back room of Kauffman Books, an open cardboard box in front of him. This morning, he'd started rummaging through the tall piles of boxes that teetered in the very back of the store, and he'd come across this boxed surprise... It was a box with sentimental items in it.

Or they would have been sentimental to a mother, or to a more loving father. Why his *daet* had kept all of this, he had no idea. There were a few crafts from his school days at the bottom of the box—a Bible verse written in cursive, a Popsicle-stick house, a mouse made out of a painted walnut shell, a lamb made out of a toilet paper tube and cotton balls... Jesse remembered making these items. He'd been particularly proud of the lamb. Except this particular lamb wasn't his. He turned it over, and inside was written *Fannie* in letters that started big and then cramped down into tiny. Back in the second grade, he and Fannie had exchanged their crafts in a spontaneous gesture.

Jesse remembered the parent night when Daet had come with him to walk around the schoolhouse, looking at all the crafts on *kinners'* desks, and when they got to Jesse's desk, his father had just looked at all of Jesse's hard work—the lamb that Fannie had made was very similar to his own, some written assignments, a colored picture—and he'd given no reaction at all. In fact, the teacher had had to hurry after them with Jesse's work in a bag, because Daet hadn't seemed inclined to take them with him.

And this was where those crafts had ended up—in a box in the storage room of the bookstore?

There were a few more items in that box: a half-knitted scarf that had never gotten long enough to actually wrap around a neck. It had been one of Fannie's early knitting efforts, and he'd told her it would make a good chest warmer. There was no such thing as a "chest warmer," but it had made her feel better, and he'd liked having something soft and comforting made by Fannie, even if it hadn't had any practical use whatsoever. It had been in his school bag, and he'd lost it. Or he'd thought he'd lost it. Maybe he'd dropped it after a school day when he was helping in the bookstore.

Had Daet meant to keep these bits of Jesse's childhood as keepsakes, or had he simply shoved them into a box and forgotten about them? Because that night in the schoolhouse, when Daet hadn't cared about his crafts, Jesse had never felt so small or insignificant. And even after, when the teacher told the class that they were making a special craft to show their parents, he refused to do it, preferring the punishment at home when the teacher told his *daet* of his disobedience to the humiliation of Daet's cold glance on parent night.

There was good reason why Jesse hadn't come back for his *daet*'s funeral. People would expect him to say kind things about his father, and Jesse hadn't been certain he could do that. His *daet* had been stern, a harsh disciplinarian and had never shown Jesse a moment of softness or tenderness. He'd never uttered the words *I love you*, and he'd never once even hinted that he was proud of anything Jesse had done.

"Why did you keep these?" Jesse muttered.

Only silence answered him, and when he glanced at the clock, he noticed it was almost five. Fannie would be off work soon, and they'd go together to the graveyard so he could see where his father had been laid to rest.

If his *daet* had lived, would Jesse have ever asked his questions? *Why didn't you love me?*

Why did you expect so much out of such a little boy? What made you so cruel?

Jesse picked up the partially finished scarf and he looked down at it for a moment. Then he put it back inside the box. Somehow, those items felt like they belonged there—a time capsule of sorts with his childhood heartbreak and his childhood comfort all wrapped up in one place. It was like his *daet* had left behind a puzzle that teased at the answers Jesse had longed to find all these years, and it left Jesse feeling irritated.

He left the box on top of the desk, and he headed out into the main shop. He shut the dampers on the woodstove and banked the fire, and put the buggy lap blankets on the top of the potbellied stove to warm up. Then he pulled on his coat and gloves, wound a scarf around his neck and then plunged outside into the winter evening.

The sun was low on the horizon. When the clocks turned back in November, sunset got even earlier. That didn't affect farmers, but it sure did affect people who worked in the shops in town. Daet used to grumble a lot about daylight saving time, and it was one thing Jesse agreed with him about. Even that small agreement didn't sit comfortably with him.

Jesse headed out to the covered stalls outside and got his horse. He had to brush some snow off his buggy before he hitched up, and there was the stable cleaning he had to do before he left, too, so he grabbed a shovel and set to work while his horse happily munched on a feedbag full of grain. Before he was finished, Fannie came around the back of the building, her black shawl pulled tight around her, and her cloth lunch bag hanging at her side.

"Just about done," Jesse called to her.

The sun had started to slip behind the hills, casting a rosy glow over the parking lot. And when he finished with the stable, he went inside to grab the lap blankets off the top of the stove, locked the shop up tight and joined Fannie in the buggy.

She was waiting for him. She shook out a warm blanket and wrapped it around her legs. She scooted closer to him, and they shared the second lap blanket between them, her warm blanket pressing against the side of his leg comfortably.

He flicked the reins and they started off.

"How was your day?" he asked.

"Good. We sold a lot of chocolate. Just before Christmas it's always so busy."

Jesse guided the horse out onto the street, and they headed away from the downtown core and toward the rosy hills.

"How was yours?" Fannie asked.

"I found a box of some of my old crafts," Jesse said. "My *daet* kept them."

"That's sweet."

"I don't know. It might have just been a mistake—shoved them into a box and forgot about them."

"He didn't toss them into the fire," she countered.

"True..."

"Why is it surprising your *daet* would keep some sweet memento of your childhood?" she asked. He glanced over and found her gray eyes fixed on him. She always coaxed the truth out of him eventually.

"Because he didn't care about those things," he replied.

"He obviously did."

"You don't understand," he said. "Daet didn't care about crafts. He cared if I got good grades, and I never really did."

"I remember you bringing your coloring pages home when we were little," she countered.

"Nope."

"You did!"

"They didn't get all the way home. I shoved them in the manure pile."

"Jesse—"

He looked over at her again, and those gray

eyes were drilling into him. "Fannie, I didn't tell you what my *daet* was like at home because I didn't want to make my father look bad. He might not have cared much about me, but I cared about him."

The truth was, when Jesse was still young enough to think he could earn some affection, he had loved his *daet*. When he got punished for something, he'd dreamed of running away and forcing his father to realize he missed him, and other days he had dreamed of doing something so heroic that his *daet* would be forced to be proud of him. But his fantasies always consisted of strong-arming his father into some sort of normal fatherly emotion.

The horse's hooves clopped against the snowy road as they headed out in the dusky evening. The sun slipped below the horizon, and the sky smudged red. Jesse flicked on his battery-operated headlights.

"What exactly happened in your home?" Fannie asked.

"I was punished a lot if I made mistakes," Jesse said, his voice wooden. "Daet had his own expectations, and I had to meet them. He never hugged me. He never did anything special for my birthday. He told me that one day I'd be glad he'd made a man of me, and I have to tell you, that day never came."

Fannie was silent, and he stole a look at her. She looked stunned. Great. That was the reaction he'd been hoping to avoid. It was partially why he'd held back filling her in. No one could believe a father would be as cruel as his had been.

"He used to ask me if I'd heard from you," Fannie said after a while. "I'd go into the bookstore and he'd let me read books if I was careful with the spines, and every time I came in, he'd ask if you'd written to me yet."

His father had asked about him? Somehow that hit Jesse in the gut. Why would his father even care what he was up to?

"Your *daet* was kind to me." Fannie's voice shook. "I was sad when he died. He used to put a little extra wood in the stove for me when I came in, and he was gruff and grumpy, but I could see past that to a little coal of goodness inside of him."

"He gave you extra wood in the stove?" he asked, incredulous.

"Yah."

Jesse couldn't imagine his father doing that for anyone. He grumbled about the price of wood, about the winter cold, about the early sunset, about the rising cost of books from the distributors, about the cost of meat, the cost of new boots and gloves for Jesse when he grew... He grumbled about everything.

"He never did that sort of thing for me," Jesse said.

"I saw a different side to your *daet*... Maybe he regretted it."

That was his boyhood fantasy—that his *daet* would regret how he'd treated his son and his *daet*'s heart would flood with love. But it wasn't realistic. Fannie slid her arm through his, and the feeling of her thick shawl against his arm was comforting.

The graveyard was on a publicly owned plot of land right next to a stretch of forest. A whitewashed wooden fence encircled it, and inside there were row upon row of plain gravestones.

Families weren't buried together like the Englishers did. They simply buried the next person who died in a row. No one was any more important than anyone else. Ironically, Jesse had felt that same sentiment from his father. Jesse hadn't been any more important to his *daet* than anyone else might have been. And it sounded like Fannie had gotten more warmth from him than Jesse had.

He pulled into the gravel parking lot and pulled the horse to a stop. His headlights shone out over the graves—rows and rows of simple Amish markers, denoting lives lived, and family members lost. He'd wanted to come see where

Daet was buried, but now that they'd arrived, he found himself frozen.

"Is that why you didn't come to his funeral?" Fannie asked, her voice low.

"Yah."

She didn't offer him platitudes or apologies, just her silent, warm presence next to him in the buggy.

"What did people say about him?" Jesse asked. He had wondered about that. What had people said in his memory?

"Your grandparents talked about him as a boy, and when he married your *mamm*," she said. "Your grandfather talked about how much your *daet* loved your *mamm*, and how they had never seen him so happy as he was in those few short years with her."

Fannie would have liked that. With her parents' marriage as her guiding light, she loved to see romance everywhere. Maybe his *daet* had loved his *mamm* that much, and maybe his grandparents were just remembering what they wanted to. Because Daet had never seemed terribly tender toward his sisters either when they came to visit once every couple of years.

"Anyone else?" His voice felt as rough as the gravel under the wheels.

"Someone mentioned that he'd given them money when they'd been in a time of hardship,"

Fannie said. "They mentioned how devoted he was to the Amish life, and how closely he followed the Ordnung."

Daet had followed the Ordnung to a T.

"Jesse, why didn't you tell me any of this?" Fannie asked.

He looked over at her, and tears sparkled in her eyes. Her lips parted and she sucked in a shaky breath. He'd hurt her by holding it all back, but he'd been trying to spare her…and to spare himself. How did he tell a girl with parents like hers that his *daet* hadn't loved him?

"It was private," he whispered.

"*Yah?* More private than all the things I told you?" she demanded. "I was your friend, Jesse! I was your best friend!"

He didn't answer, because he didn't know how to. Her words rattled around inside of him. He'd owed her more than he'd given, that was for sure and for certain.

"Maybe I wasn't your best friend," she said, amending her words. "Maybe you were closer to someone else. But you were *mine*!"

Jesse reached out and caught her hand. "You were my best friend, Fannie!"

Fannie squeezed his fingers in return, and looking down at her in the buggy, he wished he could pull her close, but their hands together were as close as they could get. At least properly. He licked his lips and looked down at their gloved fingers.

"You didn't tell me what was really happening," she said. "How could you be enduring so much and not tell me?"

"Because you were my comfort away from it all," he said, his throat tight.

"Was I?"

He looked up again to find her clear gray gaze locked on him, and his heart tumbled in his chest.

"*Yah*, you were," he said. "You would laugh and joke, and you'd tease and treat me like everything was wonderful. And when I was with you, it was."

How could he explain what she'd meant to him? But she'd also been rooted to this community, and he'd known how much he could ask of her.

"Why didn't you write, then?" Fannie asked quietly.

"I didn't write to anyone," he countered. "Just to my grandparents to give them my address the one time."

She shook her head and dropped her gaze.

"Fannie, I'm sorry." And if he could go back in time and write those letters every time he'd wanted to do it, every time he'd been desperately lonely for her, he would. But he'd been a coward—afraid she'd make him open up that painful, ugly part of his heart that he never wanted anyone to see.

"This isn't about me," Fannie said, raising her gaze once more. "You don't have to apologize to me. You needed support. You needed someone to vent to, someone who could tell you that you were worth more than the way your *daet* treated you. And I would have been that person for you!"

"It was easier to hide it," Jesse said. "I didn't want to deal with my own feelings, let alone try and explain them to someone else."

Fannie was silent for a moment, and she sucked in a slow breath. Then she nodded.

"Okay," she said.

"Okay?" What did that mean?

"*Yah.* Okay. You were dealing with a lot. You were pushing it down. I can accept that," she said.

He felt a flood of relief. She understood... Somehow, he'd been afraid he might lose her tonight, but he hadn't.

"But can I say something?" she asked.

"I don't think I could stop you," he said with a small smile.

His attempt at humor didn't touch the sober expression on her face.

"You were a good boy, Jesse. You worked

hard and you behaved well. You were such a good guy that my uncle thought you'd make good husband material for me—" She raised her gloved hand. "He was misguided. But I want to say that whatever your *daet* made you feel about yourself, you're a good man."

Somehow, her words slipped past his defenses, and unexpected tears prickled in his eyes. He blinked furiously and turned his attention toward the graveyard.

"I don't know about that," he said. "Right now, I'm a really angry man, and I'm not very good at keeping up relationships, as you found out the hard way."

"I said you were good, and I stand by it," Fannie said firmly. "Are you ready to see his grave now?"

Nee, he wasn't, but it was a cold night, and if he was going to see the grave, he'd best do it. Then, at least when he left Menno Hills, he could know he'd seen his father's last resting place.

Fannie pulled the blankets off her legs and the cold winter air made her shiver. She hopped down to the snow-covered ground, and Jesse got out on the other side of the buggy so that for a moment, she simply stood alone in the cold winter wind. Then, Jesse appeared at the horse's head and gave the animal an absent-minded stroke, his attention locked on the rows of headstones.

"Where'd they put him?" Jesse asked, his voice tight.

"Here." She led the way through the opening in the fence—the community had never bothered putting up an actual gate. Her parents were on the end of one row, side by side. Not every couple got to be buried together, and by dying in the same accident, her parents had managed it. It was a sad victory.

Jesse's *daet* was buried on the next row, just ahead of Fannie's parents. She'd put small evergreen wreaths on her parents' graves on her last visit, and she just remembered now that she'd brought one for Jesse's *daet*, too. It had been a gesture in memory of the kind bookstore owner who'd given her hundreds of new lives between the covers of those books.

Jesse squatted down in front of his father's gravestone, and he crouched there in silence. Cold wind whistled through the trees in the forest beyond, and she thought she heard the call of an owl, but it was hard to tell. The magpies imitated all sorts of noises, and they'd sit in those trees chattering like squirrels, calling like owls or making the sound of wood being chopped.

Fannie stood back, giving Jesse some space

with his feelings. Caleb had been his *daet*—the man who'd given him his height and his dark eyes. He'd raised him—for better or for worse—and fed him, and clothed him. And yet, there had been so much more going on behind closed doors that had left poor Jesse wounded and embittered.

Just a boy without any love... How had she missed that? How hadn't she noticed?

Fannie swallowed against a lump in her throat. Her parents had been wonderful. She had so many happy memories of times they had spent together as a family. They had punished her when she was wrong, but not excessively. Mostly, she'd gotten lectured and she'd felt so guilty after that she'd been determined to mend her ways from however she'd gone wrong. She'd known just how much her parents loved her, and when they'd died, she'd been bereft and adrift.

Somehow, Jesse didn't seem to be experiencing the same grief she had experienced. He looked almost like his *daet*'s death had set him free.

Jesse picked up the wreath she'd woven and tapped it against his palm.

"I left that," she said, her voice breaking the silence.

"Hmm?" He looked up.

"The wreath. I'm sorry—I left it. My way of remembering your *daet*."

"You really liked him," Jesse said, rising to his feet.

"I would have been a whole lot more conflicted if I'd known what he had put you through, Jesse."

"That's why I never said. I didn't want people to think worse of us."

"Didn't you ever consider going to the bishop?" she asked. "Bishop Moses is a wise man. He might have been able to get through to your *daet* and show him where he was going wrong."

Jesse shook his head. "*Nee*. He wouldn't have believed me...at least, I don't think he would have. It would have been my word against my *daet*'s, and my *daet* was a well-respected man. I was just a boy. I told myself I'd move away as soon as I could."

Except, he hadn't left until Ankel Moe and Caleb suggested a wedding.

"What made you run the way you did?" she asked. "Was it just the insult of them trying to foist us together?"

"Insult?" Jesse shook his head. "You weren't the insulting part. I tried explaining to him that we were friends, but Daet kept talking over me. He said I was stupid and...a lot of other things.

I'd just had enough. It was the last straw, you know? I can't say it was worse than other things he'd said to me, but he was looking down on me and he said something about how if he didn't line up a life for me, I'd never be able to do it for myself. And I just—"

Jesse didn't finish. He didn't have to. She knew exactly what he'd done. He'd packed his bags, bought a bus ticket and left town for good. No goodbye. No warning. She thought she understood. He wasn't about to be pushed into marrying Fannie, and his *daet* had touched his last nerve.

"I'm perfectly capable of putting my own life together," Jesse said, and placed the wreath back on the grave.

"You don't have to leave it there," Fannie said. "I may have overstepped."

"It's from you," he said, meeting her gaze. "My *daet* was kind to you, and you were grateful. I don't begrudge your kindness, Fannie."

But it did feel like a betrayal now. Caleb had found it in himself to be kind to her when she needed it, but he hadn't done the same for his own son.

"I'm sorry, Jesse," she said.

"For what?" he asked.

For being the recipient of his father's better intentions, perhaps, or for seeing a kind side to a man who'd hurt Jesse so deeply. It was just a tangled mess of regret inside of her.

"I don't know," she confessed. "For everything. For all of this that wasn't fair to you."

"It's not your fault," he said, softening his voice.

And she was reminded of Caleb's questions every time she went into the shop. *Has my son written to you yet? Have you heard from him?*

Maybe it was too little too late, but Caleb had missed Jesse a great deal when he left town. And maybe he would have just been angry and bitter if Jesse had come back—who knew? But in that void without Jesse, Caleb was mournful. She knew that for a fact.

But Jesse wasn't ready to hear that. He would only see it as her siding with the father who'd been so cruel to him as he was growing up, and her wreath on Caleb's grave already felt like betrayal enough.

"*Danke* for coming with me," Jesse said. "Did you want to stay longer, or are you ready to head home?"

"We can go home," she said, and Jesse reached out and caught her hand. His grip was warm and strong, and they walked together back to the buggy in the light of those headlamps.

Did he feel any better? She looked up at him,

and his gaze still looked conflicted. Maybe this visit to the graveyard wasn't going to be as healing for him as she'd hoped. But at least he'd come to see it.

When they got to the horse, they had to let go and head to opposite sides of the buggy. As she hoisted herself back up inside and covered her legs with the now-cold lap blankets, Jesse took his seat beside her.

Overhead, the stars were bright, and moonlight reflected off the snowy field.

"The first Christmas without my parents was the hardest," she blurted out.

Jesse looked over at her, and he gave her a tender smile. For a moment, he said nothing, then he gave her hand a squeeze.

"I'll be okay, Fannie."

He wasn't going to allow even a crack in his stoic strength, was he? Maybe she shouldn't be surprised. But deep inside of him, she knew that he was still aching.

Caleb Kauffman had not been as good of a man as Fannie had believed, but he was still Jesse's *daet*.

When Fannie got home that evening, the moon was high, and it was nearly two hours past the time she normally arrived. As she came into the kitchen, Aent Bethany threw her hands up.

"You're back! Fannie, I was so worried! I was about to send your *ankel* out with the buggy to look for you on the road!"

Fannie felt a surge of guilt. She of all people should know what Aent Bethany would think first—Fannie's parents had died in a buggy accident. Leaving family to worry about her wasn't considerate in the least.

"I'm sorry," Fannie said. "I should have told you I would be late. I really am sorry."

"What were you doing?" Aent Bethany asked. "Did you eat already?"

"I stopped by the graveyard on the way back," she said. With Jesse, but that didn't seem like a detail she needed to share tonight. Aent Bethany's expression softened, and she rubbed her hands over her face.

"Oh, sweetie..." Aent Bethany said.

Fannie looked out the window, watching as Jesse turned the buggy around and headed back up the drive. Her heart still seemed to be hovering outside with that buggy. She understood Jesse a whole lot better now, but all it did was make her long to comfort him in some way, to make things better for him. Jesse still seemed like a lone wolf, licking his wounds.

"Your *ankel* was hungry, so he and I ate already," Aent Bethany said. "But I have your food on the stove here. Sit down. You need a good meal in you."

Ankel Moe was probably out doing evening chores, so Fannie was alone with her aunt. Aent Bethany fetched a foil-covered plate from the top of the woodstove, and she carried it to the table. She peeled off the foil to reveal chicken cutlets, brown-buttered noodles and sauerkraut on the side. It smelled wonderful.

On the table there was a pile of local newspapers—*The Budget*, which was the Amish newspaper, and *The Menno Hills Gazette*. Fannie put the Amish paper to one side and picked up the Englisher newspaper, flipping to the back where the help-wanted postings were listed.

When her aunt passed her a fork, she put the paper aside, and bowed her head in silent grace. When she lifted her head, Aent Bethany pulled out a chair and sat down.

"This looks wonderful," Fannie said.

"I'm glad." Aent Bethany smiled. "It's cold out there. You need some food that will stick to your ribs."

"*Yah. Danke.*" She took a big bite, and for a few minutes she ate in silence, her mind running over what Jesse had told her tonight. Caleb hadn't been the man they had all thought he'd been. But Fannie had been a child and a young adult. She might not have noticed the things that adults would notice in each other.

Aent Bethany headed over to the dish rack and started to dry the dishes.

"Did you know Caleb Kauffman very well?" Fannie asked.

"Jesse's *daet*?" Aent Bethany shrugged. "I mean...we knew him. Of course, we knew him. But he was a very serious and quiet man, and we weren't particularly close friends with him. His passing has left a hole, though. I know you'll miss him at the bookshop."

"*Yah*..." Fannie nodded slowly. "I will." Although, she'd feel some guilt about that now. "He always asked me about Jesse. Every time I went in."

"The way Jesse left was rather cruel." Aent Bethany shook her head.

That was how everyone had seen it—Fannie included. But there had been a great deal more to the story.

"What was he like, though?" Fannie asked. "I was his son's age, so I didn't see what he was like with people of his own generation."

"I don't know..." Aent Bethany thought for a moment. "He was quite serious. He didn't talk a lot. He was known to report people when they didn't abide by the Ordnung. I can tell you that.

He reported Esther Mae when her *kapp* strings were too short."

"Esther Mae?"

"He was sweet on her, I think, and she rejected him," Aent Bethany said. "Oh, I feel terrible speaking ill of the dead this way! Esther Mae certainly didn't hold a grudge. Whatever mistakes he made are between him and Gott now. Not our business."

So there was another side to Caleb that others had seen...

"What are you looking for in the paper?" her aunt asked.

"Another job."

"Did something happen to the one you have?" she asked.

"*Nee*, but I talked to Esther Mae about getting more hours, and she just doesn't have them. So if I'm going to make more money, I'd best find a job that will need more of my time."

She took another bite of food and ran her finger down the help-wanted column. There were several jobs posted that were simply too far above her education level, but there were others that Fannie could do. There was a job posted at a hotel that was looking for laundry workers. Three different restaurants wanted servers. But they were all part-time, and one of the serving positions was seasonal just for the holidays.

"Fannie..." her aunt said gently.

Fannie looked up. "*Yah?*"

"You don't have to rush. It's the holiday season. Enjoy it. Besides, if you end up getting married, you wouldn't have to find a job outside of your home."

"I'm nowhere near getting married, Aent Bethany."

Her aunt nodded. "I know. But keep it in mind. I know the feeling, dear. Before I met Moe, I had given up hope. I thought it simply wouldn't happen for me. I look back on it, and it was so silly of me. I was twenty-two, perfectly pretty, could bake up a storm and utterly convinced no man would want me." She chuckled. "On this end of it, I can see how silly I was. But back then, it felt utterly hopeless. And it does feel that way, right up until you meet the right man. And then it all falls into place."

"Dieter is not the right man," Fannie said.

"Maybe not." Aent Bethany met her gaze. "But Jesse seems awfully intent on keeping Dieter at bay, too, doesn't he?"

"He thinks Dieter is a very nice man," Fannie said.

"For someone else." Aent Bethany shot her a smile. "Jesse has been sticking very close, and when your *ankel* tried to introduce you to Dieter properly, Jesse stuck by your side like a burr."

"True..." Because she'd asked him to. That was all.

"Maybe Dieter isn't the right man for you," Aent Bethany said. "And your *ankel* will not agree with me on this because he's still upset with Jesse for how he left, but you never know. Maybe Jesse has realized the opportunity he missed."

And suddenly, Fannie realized that she'd very much like Jesse to see the missed opportunity with her. She'd like nothing better than to see him finally recognize her as wife material— not just the good friend with whom he couldn't imagine any kind of romance. Because while they had been good friends, Fannie had been in love with Jesse. She'd thought that she understood him better than anyone else in his life. She'd thought she was special to him...

But she hadn't understood him at all. He'd kept the most personal, most tender part of his heart hidden away from everyone, including her, and that still hurt. Even after he had left town. Even after his insult. Even after breaking her heart!

So *yah*, she did wish that he'd finally see her the way she'd seen him all those years, but that wasn't going to happen. Jesse didn't need a wife right now, he needed an honest-to-goodness friend. And whatever she'd felt for him, whatever feelings she'd harbored that he'd never returned, Fannie had always been his loyal friend.

"It's wonderful to see Jesse again," Fannie said. "I did miss him."

She'd missed him desperately, and now that he was back, holding her heart back from him was going to be harder than she thought.

Chapter Six

The next day, the chocolate shop was particularly busy. There were several people in line to pay for their purchases, and Iris and Miriam had both tills running between them. Fannie stood at a display table, refilling it with some boxes of cream-filled chocolates molded in the shapes of bells and trees. Esther Mae was making more in the back kitchen, and the smell of tempered milk chocolate hung temptingly in the air.

As Fannie arranged the boxes, her gaze drifted toward the big display window, and out across the street. Two Englisher women wearing bright scarves and thick coats tapped on the window of Kauffman Books. She could just imagine how annoyed Jesse would be. A moment later, Jesse opened the front door and tore down a paper closed sign that he'd put up in the window. She smiled to herself.

Gott, please heal Jesse's heart.

Last night, she'd seen a different side to

Jesse—the wounded son who had never been loved half as much as he'd needed. Caleb had gone very wrong, and as kind as he was to Fannie, he'd wounded his son beyond repair, it seemed. Such bitterness. Such anger. And Jesse had just been a little boy who'd needed some understanding and love, like any child.

Was Jesse going to change his mind about dismantling the store and ending the legacy of Kauffman Books for good? She could accept that he wouldn't sell the shop to her, but the thought of Kauffman Books simply ceasing to exist still made her feel sad. She wished Jesse would run it and stay here in Menno Hills. He might have had a difficult and troubled relationship with his father, and he might have every right to the pain inside of him, but Jesse had every right to the Kauffman name, too! And... she just wanted him to stay.

Fannie turned from the window as a young Englisher man came into the store, the bell above the door tinkling merrily with a rush of cold air from outside. She stood back from the display, allowing him access to their most popular item today.

"Hi," he said, approaching Fannie. "I wonder if you could help me."

"I'll sure try," Fannie said. "What can I do for you?"

"I'm looking for a very special chocolate box," he said.

Fannie gestured to the boxes she'd just restocked. "These are very popular. They're cream filled with a delicious variety—"

"No, not like that," the young man said. "I'm proposing to my girlfriend this Christmas, and I wanted a literal box made out of chocolate that I could put an engagement ring inside of."

"Oh!" Fannie couldn't help but smile at that. "That's really wonderful! Congratulations!"

"Well, don't congratulate me yet," he said with a low laugh. "I have to ask her still. But she loves chocolate, and I always get her boxes of chocolate from your shop—it's our thing. And so I wanted to keep with the theme."

"How large of a box were you wanting?" Fannie asked.

"Maybe the size of a ring box?" he said.

She wasn't sure how big that was. The Amish didn't wear jewelry, and Fannie had never seen a ring box before.

"How big is that?" she asked, holding out her hands to show something the size of a loaf of bread.

"No, no," he laughed, and he moved her hands closer together. "Just a little square box like that—about that size. And I'd need to have something inside the box to display the ring."

An idea jumped to Fannie's mind, and she went into the display case and pulled out a larger box used for chocolate assortments, and brought it back.

"What if you had a small ring box in the center, and a whole array of chocolates surrounding it?" Fannie suggested.

The Englisher man's eyes lit up, and he nodded. "That would be perfect! I could make the proposal a bit of a surprise that way. She'd never see it coming!"

Not all surprises were so pleasant, but this one sounded delightful.

"Let me go talk to Esther Mae and see what she thinks," Fannie said.

Iris and Miriam kept ringing through the customers' orders, and Fannie went into the back of the shop to describe to Esther Mae the special little ring box this Englisher man needed. Esther Mae loved the idea, and she wiped her hands and came bustling out to talk to him. She had some immediate ideas about how to make a small box out of chocolate, and she'd even make a little crease inside the box to slip the ring into so that it would be displayed just right.

"This all sounds just perfect!" he said. "I can't thank you enough. I want to propose on Christmas Eve, so I'd need it…in a few days. Is that possible?"

"Of course. This is very important," Esther Mae said. "You might not realize this, but I pride myself on arranging some happy marriages in our Amish community. I even set up my nephew and his new wife. She's just running the till over there—the woman in pink."

"That's great," he said.

"The point is, I will do just about anything to help a couple in love," Esther Mae said with a wink. "Now, let's talk about some detailing. Would you like a few whorls and swirls on the box? And what about the surrounding chocolates? What are her favorites?"

They finished finalizing the details on the engagement order at the same time that the last of the other customers left the shop, leaving them customer-free for the moment.

"Did I hear something about an engagement?" Miriam asked.

"*Yah*, that young man is going to propose to his special friend," Esther Mae said. "It sounds like it will be quite the production, him asking her."

"He's going to do it publicly?" Iris asked.

"I'm not sure…" Fannie said. "But he wants to surprise her."

Iris winced. "I've never been engaged, so I'm no expert, but I think I'd rather have a quiet agreement with my fiancé. And I like how we keep it all a secret until just before the wedding."

"Englishers do things differently, I suppose," Fannie agreed.

"But Christmas is a lovely time to get engaged," Iris said. "Esther Mae, how did you and your husband decide to get married?"

Esther Mae's smile slipped, and she sighed. "We didn't know each other very well. He was looking for a wife, and a mutual friend introduced us."

Esther Mae must still be mourning him, Fannie realized. Sometimes, she forgot that Esther Mae had been married many years ago, but she had been. And after her husband's death, she'd opened this shop and had run it ever since.

"What time of year was it?" Fannie asked. Maybe Esther Mae would like to talk about her happy times.

"The summer, I think. I don't really remember."

"Did he ask you directly, or did you just come to an agreement?" Iris asked.

"He asked me," Esther Mae said. "But I don't like to remember these things, ladies. It was a very long time ago, and our marriage was not a happy one."

Fannie stilled, and some color came to Esther Mae's cheeks.

"I didn't mean to say that," she admitted. "I don't like to be the one who dampens happy talk. My marriage was not a good experience for me, but of course, I was raised to never speak about that."

"It might be a good idea to talk about these things," Miriam said. "How else do younger women get a warning about what to avoid?"

How did anyone know? Caleb had proven how effectively people could hide their personal cruelties from the community.

"I agree with Miriam," Fannie said. "I know we're supposed to speak well of our husbands always, but surely there are some exceptions?"

"I'd rather not scare a young woman away from marrying a man she truly loves," Esther Mae said. "You see, I do believe in marriage." She forced a smile. "I've seen enough truly happy unions—including you and Zaac, Miriam."

They were silent for a moment, and Esther Mae picked up a piece of trash from the floor and headed back toward the front counter. Fannie, Iris and Miriam exchanged uncomfortable looks. Esther Mae had been unhappy in her marriage—Fannie had never suspected that.

"Speaking of my happy home," Miriam said, looking at the clock on the wall. "I need to get home to my baby girl."

Miriam's voice sounded a little strained, and Fannie looked over her shoulder toward their boss, who was straightening up the front counter.

"Thank you so much for coming in to help today," Esther Mae said. "I truly appreciate it, Miriam. I know it's hard for you to be away from your daughter."

"My mother-in-law is delighted to babysit," Miriam said with a warm smile. "But I do miss my little Ivy."

The conversation was well and truly over, it seemed, but the discomfort was seeping away, too. Miriam gathered her things up to head home, and more customers came into the shop, chattering happily. But Fannie couldn't help but look in Esther Mae's direction while she helped a customer to fill a custom box of chocolates.

Esther Mae always seemed so strong and confident, but she'd experienced some very difficult things, too, it would seem. Much like Jesse. The Good Book said to "speak not evil one of another," and that "a whisperer separateth chief friends." Their Amish community took those admonitions against gossip seriously, especially in a marriage. A woman simply did not criticize her husband. If there was an issue to be resolved, she went to discuss it with her husband, or got help from church leadership.

But Esther Mae's husband was long dead,

and Esther Mae had kept her secrets. Jesse had done the same with his father—never breathing a word of what was happening in his home because he didn't want to speak against his *daet*. Was this silence during abuse really what Gott wanted of his people? It didn't seem to bring healing.

But with the cheery customers needing her attention, Fannie focused on serving them. Christmas was a joyful time of year, but it could be difficult, too.

May Gott provide for them all.

Jesse had been listening for the sound of Fannie's arrival for the last half hour, so when she tapped on the glass of the display window, he shot her a smile and headed over to open the door for her.

"You made it," he said. "Will you worry your *aent* and *ankel*?"

"*Nee*," she replied. "They know I'll be late." She sobered. "I need to make good use of time, though. I need to know what I'm going to do to provide for myself."

"I still think you should open a craft store," he said. "I can see you now, standing in front of some shelves with glue and glitter and beads."

Fannie laughed and rolled her eyes, and he chuckled, too.

"No craft store, Jesse. It's not happening," she said, and she hung her shawl on a coat-tree by the door. "What if I start up a bookstore?"

"Fannie's Books?" he asked.

"Maybe."

It was a little close to Kauffman's Books, though, and something inside of him rebelled at that.

"What about a card store?" he asked. "Cards and small gifts?"

"Jesse, you are impossible. I don't want to start a card shop."

"A coffee shop? Or you can give Esther Mae some competition and start up a new candy store."

He was teasing her now, like he normally had, and Fannie headed over to a shelf of dated cookbooks and pulled some volumes off a shelf, then deposited them into a box.

"Sell lumber!" he joked. "You could give the hardware store some competition and bring those prices down. If you sold nothing but lumber and nails, you could do rather well."

She cast him a rueful smile, but didn't answer.

"Are you ignoring me now?" he asked with a laugh.

"*Yah*. That's what I'm doing." She paused and looked over her shoulder at him again. "You really don't want another bookshop in town?"

"I don't know..." He squatted down in front of a box of school supplies that Daet had overstocked one year, and then never seemed to sell out of the packages of loose-leaf paper and pencils.

"Jesse."

He looked up again and found Fannie's gaze locked on him.

"This is why I didn't write," he said.

"Why?"

"You ask tough questions and don't let me sidestep them."

"So you run away from me?" She looked hurt, but not deterred. "Jesse, I'm serious. Do you really hate Kauffman Books so much that you don't even want another bookstore in the area?"

Now she was getting to the point, wasn't she? She wanted to talk about those deeper wounds, and he just wanted to keep them covered.

"I don't know!" he repeated. "I honestly don't!"

Fannie sighed and turned away again.

A medium-sized shop with shelves shouldn't be this difficult to empty out, but it was. It took more boxes than he thought to empty one shelf, and then there were the back room stock of books, the containers of bookmarks that had been shoved under the counter, the magnets, the pens.

Outside, the wind whistled between the buildings, and he felt a draft from somewhere chill his neck. Fannie shivered, too. Jesse pushed himself to his feet and went over to the woodstove in the middle of the shop. He opened the front door of the stove and pushed another two pieces of wood into the firebox, and pushed around the embers until they glowed hot and the new wood started to blacken and burn. Then he slammed it shut. He stood there, letting the heat seep into his hands and legs.

Fannie rose from her spot by the shelf and came closer to the stove. She stood at the side, and he reached out, caught her arm, and tugged her around front where most of the heat was pumping out the vents. A smile touched her lips, but she didn't look at him.

He shouldn't have said that about not writing her. It was only partly true. She did demand more of him, but his desire to run away from all these memories wasn't her fault, either.

"It's not your fault I didn't write," he admitted gruffly.

"Nee?"

"I didn't know what to say. I was so angry with my *daet* and your *ankel*, too. And I knew I owed you some sort of explanation, but I didn't have one."

"You could have said just that," she replied.

"*Yah*, well…it didn't seem like enough."

"The truth is always enough," she said.

Technically. On this side of it. But he knew Fannie, too, and she was a stickler for doing things the right way.

"You would have lectured me about forgiving my *daet*," he countered.

Fannie smiled again, but this time she looked up at him. "Probably. But you could have lectured me right back about not giving a perfectly nice farmer a chance, and we would have been even."

"You make it seem so easy," he said.

"It is easy. We've been friends a long time." She sighed. "I won't make light of it, Jesse. We were both embarrassed. We were friends, and when your *daet* and my *ankel* suggested we get married, it made us both a little bashful."

She'd hit the nail on the head there. He hadn't seen Fannie in a marrying way before, although she was his best friend. He was protective of her. He knew her better than pretty much anyone. He cared about her very much, and he missed her when she wasn't around, but their friendship was pure, and it hadn't been hiding some secret dating relationship.

"They should have just left us alone," he agreed.

"They thought they were helping," she said,

and there was something in her faint smile that made him wonder…

"You didn't want to marry me, did you?" he asked.

"You?" She laughed uncomfortably. "Of course not. You'd drive me up the wall."

"Right?" He nudged her arm. "You know it. I know it."

She glanced up at him, her eyes sad. "And I'm sure I wouldn't be your ideal, either."

Did she really want him to complain about her? He'd missed her a lot, and he was a little too grateful to have this time with her while he was in town.

"Oh, I don't know," he said. "I like your cooking. You have a razor-sharp sense of humor. You've seen me at my pettiest and my grumpiest, and you still seem to like me. I could do worse."

"That's all you want in a wife?" She laughed then, and his spirits lifted with her mirth. "I want a whole lot more than that in a husband! That's my problem."

More than him? He had half a mind to show her what she was missing.

"So what do you want?" he asked. "Do you want a handsome man?"

"I want a man who can make my heart skip a beat," she said. "I want a man whose eyes find me in a crowded room as soon as he enters. I want a man who has eyes for me and only me. And I want to feel the same way about him."

"Ah." He dropped his gaze, suddenly feeling a little embarrassed. He recognized himself in one of her items on her wish list. "I mean, I always look for you when I arrive at a singing, or at some gathering."

He wanted her to know that. She did have a man in her life who preferred her company over anyone else's.

"You do?" Her voice quavered.

"*Yah.*" He shrugged. "I need to know if you're there so I can catch you on your way out. Or... I don't know...look over at you when Elder Ben starts mentioning the weevils in the flour of our hearts."

Fannie's eyes glittered with humor, then a smile broke over her face. "Last month, it was the locusts in the fields of our community unity."

"*Yah?*" He laughed. "Elder Ben does love his insect illustrations. And who else would find that as funny as I do?"

"Not Deacon Michael," she said, casting him a coy little smile.

He barked out a laugh. The last time he had snickered at an insect story, Deacon Michael had given Jesse a talking-to about being serious and sober, and looking for the meaning behind the words, not laughing at the surface.

And Deacon Michael had been absolutely right, of course. But Jesse had been remembering jokes he and Fannie had made, so his laughter hadn't really been about Elder Ben's very serious story about a beetle, after all.

"But that's important," Jesse said. "Before you marry a man, you'd better make him listen to Elder Ben talk for at least half an hour. If he doesn't snicker even once, then I forbid you to marry him."

"Forbid me?" she snorted.

"I forbid it!" He gave her a look of mock severity, and then they both laughed.

"You can't forbid me anything," she laughed.

"Wait, I'm not done!" he said, turning toward her. "I also require you marry a man who is perfectly okay with you making me those delicious lemon tarts on my birthday."

"What man will be okay with that?" she shot back.

"The right one." He arched an eyebrow at her. "Also, he needs to go busy himself with other conversation while you and I go over the latest pest-related sermon analogy."

"You really think you're going to get all that?" Fannie retorted with a laugh. "You're awfully silly, Jesse. The man I marry is going to chase you off with a stick, I can tell you that much."

"Then you can't marry him," he replied with a grin. "Having me around has to be your deal-breaker."

He was only kidding around, of course, but even mentioning her marrying some man was getting under his skin, so he had to make a joke of it. Her husband would definitely want to see the back of Jesse, and he knew it. For good reason.

"So that's it—I need to tell a man he has to let me have my male best friend in my life in exactly the same way he's always been, or I won't marry him?" she asked.

"You could try..." He sobered. "Remember when we were twelve and we promised each other we'd never marry anybody and we'd just run wild for the rest of our days?"

"I lied," she whispered.

"What do you mean, you lied? That was a very solemn promise..." His words were joking still, but he lowered his voice to a rumble.

"I promised you I'd never marry anyone, but in my heart I told myself I'd marry you."

Jesse stilled. She'd wanted to marry him? Gangly, acned and accident-prone as he'd been? She'd wanted to marry him? The thought was both surprising and sweet.

"Obviously, I outgrew that little flight of fancy," Fannie said with an uncomfortable laugh. She turned away.

"Obviously..." he murmured. "Fannie, did I miss something back then?"

"How I felt about you?" she asked softly.

He nodded, unsure of how to put it. Had she been in love with him and he'd never noticed? Was he really that thick?

"A little bit," she said.

He was stunned. Fannie had felt more for him? If he'd known that, he might have thought about it more seriously. He'd thought she only saw him as a brother or a pal. He'd never guessed that she might see something worthy of marriage and commitment in him.

"I thought we were just buddies," he said, trying to explain. "I didn't think there was more— I thought that—"

"There wasn't more," Fannie said, cutting him off. "We were only friends, Jesse, but I did harbor some feelings I never said out loud. That's the truth of it. I never wanted to tell you, and I never intended to. But since you asked me so directly, I don't want to lie."

"Maybe you should have told me," he said. "Apparently, I'm not very good at relationships. You should know that by now."

"I should have told you and ruined our friendship?" She shook her head. "You ran fast enough when someone else brought it up. No, Jesse, we were friends."

But the warmth in the room, and the soft pinging of the heat going up the stovepipe had taken the humor out of him, and Jesse looked down at Fannie's gray eyes, looking almost charcoal in the low evening light. A single eyelash lay on her cheek, and he touched it with the tip of his finger and then blew it away with a puff of breath. And suddenly, he found himself looking at her lips. They were slightly parted, and Fannie was so close, smelling faintly of sweet chocolate, and Jesse found himself thinking that she'd marry someone eventually, and some other man would be kissing those lips. The very thought made him want to throw this imaginary husband out a window. Fannie hadn't been his girlfriend, but she'd been his.

He'd never seen Fannie as more than a friend before this, although of course he knew she was a woman. But there was something about her this evening that made him ever so aware of the way her eyes sparkled in the low light, and how the warmth from the woodstove was making her cheeks flush pink.

Fannie was gorgeous...and more than anything, he wanted to kiss her. He wanted to pull her close into his arms, feel the heat of the stove from the fabric of her dress, and cover those pink lips with his own...

A rap on the window startled him, and Jesse looked over his shoulder to see Steven Browning, a local Englisher business owner. He waved a gloved hand.

"Uh—" Jesse licked his lips. "I'd better see what he wants."

"*Yah*, of course." Fannie took a big step back and rubbed her hands over her arms.

Jesse's head was still feeling a little light, and he unlocked the front door.

"Jesse!" Steven said. "It's really good to see you."

"Come inside," Jesse said, stepping back. Steven came in with a rush of cold air, and Jesse was glad to slam the door shut again.

"I'm so sorry about your father's passing," Steven said. "Truly."

"*Danke*," he replied. "I mean, thank you."

"The reason I'm here tonight is we've got a community event happening tomorrow. We'll have hot cocoa, and caroling, and some wagon rides. We're collecting food for the food bank, and there will be gifts for the children. It was really popular last year."

"Sounds great," Jesse said.

"The thing is, the Amish men are driving the wagons for the wagon rides through town to see all the Christmas lights, and Johanns Miller has the flu. His wife just let us know. So we need another wagon driver. Any chance you'd be willing?"

Jesse rubbed his hand over the back of his neck, thinking for an excuse. Did he really feel up to that much Christmas cheer right now?

"I've got a lot to get done here in the shop—" he started.

"It's just one evening," Steven said. "And it would help us out a lot."

Jesse glanced over his shoulder toward Fannie. She had gathered up a few more books in her arms and when he met her gaze, she gave him a faint shrug.

"I think it might be good for you to get out amongst people a little bit," Fannie said.

She was probably right. Cooped up in this shop with nothing but memories wasn't good for him, either.

"*Yah*, sure," Jesse replied. "Just for one evening."

"Thank you so much," Steven said, shaking Jesse's hand heartily. "And Merry Christmas to both of you."

"Merry Christmas," Jesse replied, and when he'd shut the door behind Steven, he looked back at Fannie.

"It's good for you," Fannie said. "And I need to get home. I think it's late enough, don't you?"

"You want to go home already?" he asked.

Fannie looked up at him miserably. "I probably should."

"*Yah*, sure. I can drive you back," he replied. Of course, he'd take her if that was what she wanted. She was embarrassed that she'd said so much, and maybe he was foolish for having asked her about what she'd felt way back then. He'd ruined the evening.

Fannie was right, though. Any more time alone with her tonight, and he was liable to do something he'd probably regret.

In some ways, two years hadn't changed a thing. He and Fannie still felt like two peas in a pod. But other things had changed…like just how pretty Fannie was when she was telling him straight what she thought.

If his *daet* hadn't put his nose into Jesse's personal life, Jesse might have gotten to the point of seeing Fannie differently all on his own. But as it was, Daet had butted in, and Jesse didn't want anything from his father—least of all a setup.

Chapter Seven

Sitting next to Jesse on the way home in his buggy felt different than it had before. Somehow, every other buggy ride with a lap blanket shared between them had felt more like a buggy ride with a brother or a cousin—men she could laugh and joke with without complication.

But something had happened in the bookstore. She'd said too much, and now when Jesse glanced over at her, he wasn't looking at her the same way he usually did. His gaze was a little softer, a little more thoughtful. And that wasn't really fair. Fannie had already made her peace with the dynamic of their friendship. They were pals. They were supportive of each other—or had been until Jesse had left town so abruptly. Sure, she'd known just how handsome Jesse was. But he was more than good looks. He was kind, too, and funny. No one could make her laugh like Jesse. But he wasn't *hers*. Not like that.

So looking at Fannie the way he was looking at her tonight wasn't fair at all. Because if Jesse had jumped at the chance to marry her when her uncle and his father had suggested it, Fannie would have married him in a heartbeat.

Not that she'd tell him that.

"Why are you looking at me that way?" Fannie asked.

Jesse turned his gaze quickly back toward the road. "What way?"

"You're being weird," she said, unsure of how else to describe it.

A smile turned up his lips, but he kept his eyes on the road, all the same.

"Am I going to regret driving a wagon for the town's Christmas festival?" he asked.

"Only if your heart is an icicle," she said with a laugh. "It's good to enjoy the holiday season. The Englishers love it, and they'll keep you fed with cookies and hot cocoa. You won't suffer."

"How come you don't feel sorry for me?" he asked, and she heard the joking in his tone. "You should have a little pity."

"You don't deserve pity," she replied. "You have family and community right here. You don't have to go off by yourself."

Jesse had *her* right here—again, not something she'd say.

"Will you come along on the wagon ride with me?" he asked.

"Why should I?" she asked, just to be difficult, but she gave him a coy little smile, all the same.

"Because you like me?" he asked hopefully.

"I do like you," she said. "I have to work tomorrow at the chocolate shop. It's going to be busy, and we're handing out free chocolate samples on the street."

"So when you're finished work, then," he said.

"I suppose I could do that." But she was pleased he asked her. Jesse could be as daft as a stunned steer sometimes, but she had a very hard time refusing him anything he asked her for. Besides, Jesse, as always, was her soft spot. It came with the familiar territory of being halfway in love with her best friend.

Jesse pulled into the drive, and Fannie gathered up her lunch bag. Everything looked ordinary in their drive—the stable closed up tightly against the night cold and light shining in a welcome glow from the first-floor windows. Normally, only the kitchen would be lit up, but perhaps her *ankel* was reading or something in the other room.

"*Danke* for the ride, Jesse," she said.

"See you tomorrow after work?" he asked.

"*Yah*, I'll go with you on your wagon ride," she said.

"It'll be fun," he said.

It would be, she had to admit, and with another smile, she hopped out of the buggy and headed up the steps and into the house.

"Hello, Fannie!" Aent Bethany called. "You're home a little earlier than I thought."

"I thought I should come back," Fannie replied. "I didn't eat out like I thought I might, so I'm hungry."

"Good, because there are leftovers," Aent Bethany said, and she pulled a foil-covered plate off the stove. "Even if you did eat, with that cold out there, I thought you'd want a little more."

Aent Bethany did believe in fueling a body against the cold, and Fannie gratefully accepted the plate of food. Just then, Ankel Moe came in from the sitting room, followed by Dieter Glick.

Fannie's heart hammered in her throat, and her aunt cast her an apologetic look. Fannie hadn't seen an extra buggy in the drive. Had she seen one, she would have asked Jesse to drive with her a little longer...or maybe to bring her back to see his *mammi* and *dawdie*. But this was a dirty trick. Where was Dieter's telltale buggy?

"You're back from work, Fannie," Ankel Moe said jovially. "I'm glad. Dieter came by for a visit this evening. I'll drive him back to the Yoders' place in a little while."

That explained it. He hadn't driven on his own.

"I don't want to miss my youngest daughter's bedtime," Dieter said. "Hello, Fannie. It's nice to see you again. How was work?"

Aent Bethany put Fannie's plate on the table.

"Uh—" Fannie smiled hesitantly. "It was fine. The holiday season is always busy."

"Don't let me keep you from eating," Dieter said, gesturing to the table. "It's a delicious meal. We just finished."

Fannie slid into the seat and looked down at the plateful of various dishes—noodles, cabbage, sausage, potatoes, steamed carrots. Her stomach rumbled. She was hungry, in spite of it all.

Well, maybe she could put Dieter off by simply eating in front of him. She bowed her head for a short grace, and then took a bite. Dieter pulled up a chair a couple of seats away—not too close—and he had a friendly enough look on his face. She noticed the gray in his beard—just a few strands—but his face looked closer to her uncle's age. That was hard to get around.

Fannie swallowed and took another bite.

"Do you enjoy working at the chocolate shop?" Dieter asked.

She nodded, still chewing, and Aent Bethany gave her an exasperated look. Well, Dieter had said he didn't want to keep her from her meal!

"Do you know Iris Bischel?" Fannie asked once she could politely speak again.

"I do. We went to school together," Dieter replied, sounding a little surprised. "Do you know her?"

"Of course," Fannie replied. "We work together at Black Bonnet Amish Chocolates."

"I didn't realize that," he replied. "I thought she was teaching or something."

"*Yah*, she's worked at the chocolate shop longer than I have," Fannie replied. "And she teaches volleyball, too."

"Huh. That's interesting," he murmured.

"What was she like in your school days?" Fannie asked. Somehow, talking about Iris seemed easier than anything else. Dieter smiled and shrugged. His face softened.

"She used to tease me ruthlessly," Dieter said.

"What? Iris?" Aent Bethany interjected.

"*Yah*. She might look calm and sweet, but she's got a sharp sense of humor," Dieter said. "I was very skinny back then—hadn't really hit my growth spurt—and she used to bring me jelly doughnuts and tell me that she felt obliged to feed me."

That sounded like Iris had been flirting more than teasing, Fannie thought, but she had noticed how Dieter had relaxed when he spoke about his old school friend, and talking about Iris felt like much safer territory.

"What else did she do?" Fannie asked.

"She used to put these scratchy little pine cones down the back of my neck," Dieter said. "And she beat me in every foot race. Until I grew, at least, and then she refused to race me because it wasn't ladylike." He grinned ruefully. "She just didn't want to lose to me."

Dieter and Iris's dynamic sounded a lot like the way Fannie and Jesse used to horse around together.

"You were good friends," Fannie said.

"*Yah*, we were." Dieter nodded. "Has she mentioned me?"

"Not much," Fannie murmured, and she took another bite. She couldn't very well tell him that Iris had been encouraging this match.

"But she's not Iris Bischel anymore, is she?" Dieter asked. "She got married, right?"

Fannie and Aent Bethany both shook their heads at the same time, but Fannie's mouth was full, so her aunt answered.

"No, she was going to get married about ten years ago, but the engagement fell through," Aent Bethany said.

"Why? What happened?" Fannie asked, swallowing.

"He didn't stay Amish," Aent Bethany said. "At least he had the courtesy to tell her before he married her. She wasn't willing to go English with him, and so the wedding was called off."

This was all news to Fannie. She hadn't known Iris beyond her name until she began working with her at the chocolate shop. Iris never spoke about her broken engagement, but it was sad that Iris had missed out on her life of married happiness that way.

"I'd wanted to visit a little longer, but I'm looking at the time—" Dieter eyed the clock on the wall "—and I really need to get back to get my littlest to bed. It's something that matters to me—I always tuck them in."

"Of course," Fannie said. "You're a good *daet*." And she couldn't help but approve of a man prioritizing his *kinner* that way.

"Do you mind if we head out, Moe?" Dieter asked.

"Not at all," Ankel Moe said, and he gave Fannie a fond smile. "I'm glad you could visit for a while."

It didn't take long for the men to head outside together, and when the door clapped shut behind them, Fannie cast her aunt a wary look.

"Go ahead," Fannie said. "Lecture me about being rude enough to eat in front of him."

"No, I think he liked that you were comfortable," Aent Bethany said with a smile.

Not quite the response that Fannie was going for, but she had to agree. Dieter hadn't been put off by her eating her meal one bit.

"I didn't know about Iris's engagement," Fannie said.

"*Yah*, she was crushed," Aent Bethany said. "She was really in love with him, and it was a very difficult choice for her. We all assured her she'd find another man, but it didn't work that way."

"She has a very full life working at the chocolate shop and coaching the girls' volleyball team in town," Fannie said. "She's made such a difference in those girls' lives. They all adore her."

"Life is not over because a woman doesn't have a husband," Aent Bethany agreed. "But if I were to give you a tiny piece of advice?"

"Sure."

"Don't mention other single women when a man is interested in you, dear," Aent Bethany said. "That might be a little counterproductive. Iris might be older than you, but she isn't exactly out of the running when it comes to Dieter Glick."

Fannie didn't answer, but it did occur to her that another good way to dissuade Dieter from being interested in her was to turn his attention to someone else. And she'd recognized something rather special in the way that Dieter smiled when he talked about Iris.

It was the exact smile Jesse got on his face when he talked about their school days. And Fannie knew just how precious a friendship like that was.

***

The Menno Hills Christmas Festival started at noon sharp. There was a marching band playing a noisy Christmas carol medley—they were from the local high school—and a live-action Nativity scene in the snowy yard in front of the Presbyterian church. Some carolers dressed in Victorian-era clothing were walking up and down Church Street singing "God Rest Ye Merry Gentlemen," which clashed with the marching band, and there were some street carts—one selling hot pretzels with hot cheese sauce, and another one selling coffee and tea.

Jesse had to admit that it was a rather cheery scene. Not very Amish, either. The Amish celebrated Christmas in a more thoughtful and reflective way. This was the sort of local event that his *daet* would have hated, which was partly why he was willing to take part in it.

Jesse stood next to the draft horse that was all hitched up to a wagon. The horse's breath hung in the cold winter air, and he shook his mane, making the bells on his harness jingle. But Jesse found himself looking toward the chocolate shop as customers came and left.

He'd almost kissed his best friend last night, and he wasn't sure what had happened. But something inside of him had changed when he looked at Fannie Flaud, and he was pretty sure that wasn't a good thing. As friends, he and Fannie knew exactly where they stood. If he started feeling more for her, he was going to be toying with some very powerful emotions, and he'd likely ruin his friendship with her for good.

But he'd almost kissed her! And if Steven hadn't shown up when he had, Jesse would have had a whole lot to apologize for today. That was a sobering thought.

"Jesse Kauffman," a voice said next to him, and he looked over to see Elder Ben standing there, a grimace on his face. He knew that look. The old man was disapproving of something.

"How are you, Elder Ben?" Jesse said.

"I'm not sure I approve of all this jingling and jangling," Elder Ben said. "I have half a mind to discuss this with the bishop. The town wants us Amish to participate, but I'm not sure this is even proper. The quiet Christmas plans they told us about have gotten all out of hand!"

Jesse glanced around. Fannie came out of the chocolate shop dressed in her shawl and bonnet, a platter of chocolate samples held out in front of her, and he waited to see if she'd notice him. She didn't. Some Englisher children crowded around her, hoping for a chocolate.

"It might be a little English, I'll admit," Jesse said. "But it's cheery, and right now, I could use a little cheer."

Elder Ben's expression froze, and then dropped. He met Jesse's gaze earnestly.

"Jesse, I wasn't even thinking of your loss," the old man said. "Forgive me for that."

Jesse blinked. "Of course."

"Here I was thinking of propriety and those silly carolers down the way, and the donkey for the Nativity scene that keeps trying to make a run for it, and…" He reached out and put a gloved hand on Jesse's shoulder. "How are you doing, Jesse?"

"Uh—" Jesse was caught off guard. "I'm doing pretty well."

At least with Fannie back in his life, things were feeling better than they had since he'd heard the news that his *daet* had passed away.

"Your *daet* was a good man, and he'll be missed," Elder Ben said quietly. "I'm truly sorry that you lost him so young, Jesse. Truly."

Everyone said the same things.

"*Danke.*" It was a safer answer.

Elder Ben looked around the street just as the marching band started up a blasting rendition of "Away in a Manger" that would wake the dead, let alone a baby.

"I'll complain to the bishop later. Enjoy some distraction, young man."

"No pest analogy?" Jesse asked with a wry smile.

"What?" Elder Ben frowned. There was the clash of a set of cymbals, and the band marched on past, boots splashing in the slushy street.

Jesse felt a stab of guilt. He'd made light of the older man's words of wisdom over the years, and here Ben was being downright decent to him.

"It's just—" Jesse had to explain himself now. "You always tie it in to grasshoppers or ants or hornets somehow. Sorry—I don't mean to be rude, Elder Ben."

"Did you want me to tie it in to Gott's creation?" Elder Ben asked, his white eyebrows raised.

And Jesse realized he really did want to hear what the old man would say.

"Please," he said.

"The honeybee can only sting once," Ben said soberly. "But it has a very important job to do in pollinating flowers and crops. But sting it will, if threatened. We often forget that people are the same—they have one big panic inside of them before everything changes forever. We should be gentler with each other."

A lump rose in Jesse's throat. Had he had his own big panic of a lifetime already when he had headed out of town and started over in Indiana? Suddenly, Elder Ben's insect metaphors didn't seem quite so humorous anymore.

Elder Ben patted his shoulder. "It's good to see you at home, Jesse."

"It's good to see you, too, Elder Ben," he replied.

The old man headed off down the sidewalk, giving Fannie a brisk shake of his head when she proffered him the platter of chocolate samples. Fannie looked up and caught Jesse's gaze quizzically. He just shrugged.

An explanation for another time.

Some Englishers came over to the wagon, looking at him hopefully.

"Hop on up," Jesse said. "We'll start out in a few minutes."

The day passed quickly enough. The locals were excited about the wagon rides, and Jesse took them slowly down Church Street so they could see the Nativity display with the donkey that kept trying to escape, then down another street of shops that had all their lights and baubles on display. He stopped for a Santa Claus who was handing out candy canes, declining one for himself, and then took his chattering, happy passengers down along a street of houses that had their lawns decorated with everything from inflatable snowmen to one house that had a whole Nativity scene made out of wicker.

The Amish didn't decorate like this. It seemed

so over-the-top to Jesse. His grandmother would light some white pillar candles, and she'd decorate with some red berries from a tree outside, and some evergreen sprigs. The smell of spruce sap and candle wicks always put him in a Christmas mood. But he could see why Englishers enjoyed this bigger display. There was something irrepressibly joyous about all this lawn decor.

He had to wonder what Fannie thought of it... She kept slipping into his thoughts these days, more than usual even. He cared what she thought, what she was feeling. He'd been thinking about that moment by the woodstove an awful lot, too, and wondering what he would have done had Stephen not knocked.

She'd said she'd had feelings for him in the past...did that mean she felt more for him now? Or had she wised up?

The evening drew on, and the temperature dropped. Jesse gladly ate a toasted sandwich he bought from a vendor, and drank a large cup of hot chocolate while he stood next to the horse and waited on his next load of passengers.

Fannie came out of the shop then, dressed in her woolen shawl and her bonnet. Her cheeks were pink—the only color he could see—and Jesse pulled out an extra sandwich he'd bought for her. He waggled it at her, and a smile split over her face. He loved that he could make her grin like that. He also remembered her favorite toasted sandwich—Philly cheesesteak.

Fannie accepted the sandwich with a smile and tore open the paper to take her first bite. She sighed in satisfaction.

"I needed this," she said.

"Thought so," he replied.

She ate quickly, and wiped off her fingers with the napkin as an Englisher family loaded up into the wagon.

"Are you enjoying the wagon driving?" Fannie asked.

"The lights are coming on now on the streets," Jesse said. "You're just in time."

When the Englishers had piled onto the bench seats, Jesse gave Fannie a hand up onto the front seat, then hoisted himself up next to her. He'd been looking forward to her joining him tonight, and he found himself smiling in spite of himself.

"So, just for the record, we're still putting on a nice show of me courting you, right?" he said.

Fannie blinked at him. "*Yah*, I guess we are."

"Good." He spread the lap blanket over both of their knees, then flicked the reins. The big draft horse leaned into the weight of the wagon and started forward at an easy, plodding pace, the sound of his hooves muffled against the snowy street.

"Dieter came by our place last night," Fannie said.

A rush of annoyance surged through Jesse that he had little right to, but he felt it all the same. Dieter was persistent, wasn't he? And maybe Jesse could understand. Fannie was worthy of some pursuit, but she wasn't interested in the older man.

"Without an invitation?" he asked. Was Dieter pushing himself on a much younger woman?

"Well, he was visiting with my *ankel*," she said.

"How did that go?" he asked, trying to keep his voice neutral. What he wanted to ask was did Dieter force the issue, insist that he be able to visit with a woman who had no interest in visiting with him. Jesse didn't like the thought of Fannie being put in these awkward positions by all the older adults around her. That wasn't fair.

"We actually had a nice talk," she replied.

"*Yah?*" he eyed her uncertainly.

"Like you said before, he's a nice man."

"I know I said it, but I might change my mind about that," he said irritably.

"He was fine, actually," Fannie said. "He knows Iris Bischel from his school days."

He raised his eyebrows. The name was familiar, but he didn't know her personally.

"Iris is older than we are," Fannie said. "I work with her at the chocolate shop. She's single."

"Okay..."

"And in the course of Dieter's visit, I found out what happened to Iris. She was engaged, but her fiancé went English."

"Oh..." This seemed to be a rather important detail to Fannie, but he couldn't see why. Did that make her like Dieter more or less? How on earth did Dieter's schoolmates factor into her situation at all?

"She was really heartbroken, my *aent* says. Aent Bethany remembers when it happened, but I don't think I ever knew. They didn't have their banns announced or anything. But here's the good part," Fannie said. "Iris and Dieter were very good friends. Friends like you and me. And—" Color touched her cheeks, then, and she stopped.

"And?" he prompted.

"You're going to say I'm silly," she said. "But I saw the way he lit up when he talked about her, and I think there's a possibility that they might make a very good match."

Friends like they'd been... He felt a little bit of warmth touch his cheeks. Jesse might have been a little daft, but their friendship had been a very special one.

"You aren't going to try and lead them together?" Jesse asked with a low laugh.

Fannie shot him an annoyed look. "It would certainly take care of my problem."

"Are you going to do anything about it?" he asked.

"When you plant a seed, you don't go digging it up and replanting it. You cover it over, and leave it alone. I'm not foolish enough to bother with it again. I know what I saw, and Dieter Glick has some very fond memories of Iris."

"And those fond memories…"

"Are more than he's got with me!" she said. "I think they could very well be a foundation."

Somehow, it made Jesse feel better to know that Fannie was still plotting her own freedom. He wasn't sure why, but having Fannie settle down with a very nice man whom she didn't love was downright angering. Would he feel better if she loved the man? No, he wouldn't. He'd just feel a whole lot more jealous.

And when Jesse looked over at Fannie sitting next to him, her hands on her lap, the blanket covering her knees, and the Christmas lights approaching ahead, he suddenly felt a fresh rush of tenderness toward her.

"We're supposed to be courting, right?" he said.

"*Yah*, of course."

He reached over and caught her gloved hand in his. "Is this okay?"

In answer, she scooted closer to him on the bench seat, and he felt a wave of relief flood through him—and he wasn't even sure why. But it felt right to have her hand in his, and he was glad to be the man at her side tonight. Let the whole community talk. Let them gasp and whisper, but Fannie Flaud was worth having a man publicly court her. No one seemed to realize just how wonderful Fannie was. If they did, they wouldn't be suggesting her for an older man with five *kinner* already. They'd be lining up their sons for her.

So maybe before he left, he could help the community to see what he saw in Fannie.

Just not Dieter Glick. Dieter might be a perfectly nice man, but something inside of Jesse wanted to elbow the man out of the way.

But he was starting to wonder if he might be able to help Fannie get an even bigger escape than the one he was already providing. What if she came with him to Indiana? Was that foolish of him to even think about?

Chapter Eight

The passengers in the wagon oohed and aahed, and took pictures and videos with their phones. Fannie and Jesse didn't have phones to record the light display, of course, but Fannie did lean forward for a better view, watching all the glitter and dancing lights.

The evening was now dark enough that the Christmas lights in Menno Hills' residential areas were on full display. The street they took the passengers down was dubbed Christmas Lane by the town of Menno Hills, and the owners along that stretch of housing took extra care in putting up their displays. Lights glowed, flickered and rolled. One house had a Santa Claus laughing with a tinny voice from a life-size sleigh. One house had large, glittering snowflakes that danced from tree branches, interspersed with large Christmas balls.

"It's pretty, I have to admit," Fannie said in Pennsylvania Dutch.

"*Yah*, it is," he agreed. "The bishop and elders will probably talk about the Amish taking part next year, though. It's gotten so much…fancier."

It had. Every year it got a little more sparkly, a little more English. Amish wagons and Amish food were always welcome additions, but not the Amish dedication to simplicity and plainness. It was exciting and fun, but with more sparkle, there was a little less peace, too.

"What is your community in Indiana like?" she asked.

"It's a little more modern," he said. "We are allowed to have electric heaters in our buggies, and electricity in our barns."

"Oh!" That sounded almost English to her. How much had Jesse changed?

"It's just a more liberal community," he said. "But with more permissiveness comes more responsibility, and they guard the Ordnung very closely."

"You don't miss Menno Hills?" Fannie asked.

He was silent for a few beats, and Fannie thought she knew what that meant.

"I miss you." He glanced over at her, his eyes sad.

But not enough to write, and not enough to come back. Fannie turned forward again, watching the big draft horse slowly plod down the snowy street, tail swishing as he walked.

"You know, you should come visit," Jesse said. "I've been thinking about it. I think you'd like it out there."

"I don't know if I'd be able to adjust to more modern ways," she said. "My *daet* always said that we do things the way we do to keep us closest to Gott. With more luxuries, we start to drift."

"There's less frostbite," Jesse said. He was trying to joke.

She shot him a wry look.

"I know, I know," he said with a laugh. "But it doesn't take away from the community's focus on Christian living. They have made some allowances for safety and some comfort during winter, but they don't budge on the things that matter. I really think you'd like it there."

Except all of her memories were here. Her parents' graves were here, and her cousins, and aunts and uncles. Her roots were here.

"I'm not moving away from Menno Hills," she said.

"I didn't say to move," he countered. "I said you should visit."

That stung, somehow. He wasn't asking for anything permanent.

"Go visit you to what end?" she asked. "Just to see where you prefer to live?"

"Fannie…"

Fannie knew she was being difficult. They were friends, and friends visited each other. But they were also a man and a woman, and if she went to visit him in Indiana, people would make assumptions. It could hurt both of their reputations.

"I'm not just a pal," she said, looking down at her hand in his. "I'm a woman."

"I know." His voice dropped. "But you're special."

"Not that special. You're not really courting me. Me going to see you in your new community without us being engaged could hurt both of us."

Jesse was silent for a moment. "I guess I forget this isn't real."

He wasn't the only one.

"Well...don't forget it," she said, trying to keep her voice light. She tugged her hand out of his. They were supposed to be fooling her *ankel* and *aent*, and anyone else who might try to push her into a marriage she didn't want. They weren't supposed to be fooling themselves.

Fannie felt a little colder as they carried on down the street. She shouldn't be sad that her friend missed her. And she shouldn't be upset that he wanted to see her after he went back. It was certainly a step up from his disappearing act two years ago. He cared—that was what she'd wanted to know all this time, wasn't it? That he cared?

Why wasn't that enough for her right now? Because it wasn't anymore.

Finally, they arrived with their wagonload of chattering passengers back to the spot where they had begun. The horse plodded up to Black Bonnet Amish Chocolates, and Jesse reined him in. The horse shook his head, giving a shiver of bell tinkles into the winter night. The passengers were standing up, talking amongst themselves about the beauty of the night, and Fannie noticed an Englisher man standing across the street in front of Kauffman Books. He wore a woolen winter coat, blue jeans and a plaid scarf around his neck. He perked up when he saw the wagon, and he looked both ways before he jogged across the street toward them.

"Hello!" the Englisher called out. "Jesse!"

Jesse turned toward him, then waved.

"Do you know him?" Fannie asked.

"*Yah*. That's Dave Morton. He runs a used bookstore in Vinton. Just give me a minute. This might be promising."

Jesse hopped down, went around to the back of the wagon and lowered the stairs so that the people could descend. They chattered as they got down into the street, and Jesse turned to talk to the Englisher. She could hear a few words between the men that weren't drowned out by the Victorian carolers who were standing at the corner singing "Good King Wenceslas."

But then the carolers finished their song, and she could hear what the men were saying more clearly.

"I need to unload them before Christmas."

"I heard you were emptying your shop, so I took the chance to come see you. One of your Amish friends said you were driving a wagon and were due back. I'm glad I caught you."

"What are you interested in buying? Shelves? A till? I have rolls of receipt paper—everything has to go."

"I want nonfiction books—whatever you've got."

"A lot of it is theological," Jesse said.

"I've got customers for that, but I can't give you a lot. I have to sell them as used books—"

"What about a hundred dollars a box?"

"Fifty."

"Fine. Fifty. Deal?"

"Deal."

No more haggling than that? Some of those books could be sold on the shelf at a hundred dollars apiece! Fannie had spent enough time in the shop to know the prices of almost all of those books. Some of them were worth a lot more. A whole box for the retail price of one book? That Englisher had just taken advantage of Jesse, and by the smug look on Dave's face, he knew he'd just gotten those books for a steal. It was wrong. The men shook hands, and Fannie realized she'd been staring when Jesse turned back toward her.

"You're selling the books by the box?" she asked breathlessly.

Jesse caught her arm and pulled her a little farther away from listening ears.

"I need to empty the store," he said, his voice low.

"That's well below cost!" she said. "Your *daet* collected those books over years—"

But bringing his *daet* into this was a mistake, and she knew it as soon as the words left her mouth, because Jesse's expression hardened.

"I have to empty the store," Jesse repeated. "And I'm on a timeline here. He's willing to come pick them up himself."

So this Dave Morton had made a very good deal for himself to sell those books in his own store. Those beautiful, sometimes rare, books were simply going to be carted out, and Fannie felt almost lightheaded. She'd known what he was planning on doing, but watching it happen was a whole other thing!

Jesse would rather sell the books at an insulting loss than sell them to her?

"Jesse, those books are worth much more," Fannie said, keeping her voice low. "If you were at least trying to get as much money as possible for them, I'd understand. But you aren't opening the shop before Christmas. You aren't even advertising a big sale. You're almost giving them away!"

"It doesn't matter—"

"Those books are worth more! They're—they're like oxygen to some people. Do you know that? They let you breathe when your whole life is closing in on you."

Her breath came fast, and she looked into his face, hoping for some understanding. Did he know what books could do for a person? They could be her lifeline. They could give her hope when her whole world had caved in on her.

Jesse was silent for a moment, then he shook his head. "I'm sorry, Fannie. I am. But I have to empty the place. You know that."

Yah, but now she had to watch him do it. And he wouldn't sell it to her and let her protect what was left of that shop. He didn't understand at all.

"You might as well just pile everything up on the curb and let the garbage collectors take it!" she said. "Jesse, I understand that you don't want to run that shop, but that doesn't mean your *daet* didn't build up something worthwhile. I *loved* that store!"

She had spent hours inside of it, losing herself in books, finding herself in those same pages. She'd read stories about women who'd hurt just like she had and who had still built beautiful lives for themselves. She'd read about love, determination, faith and resilience.

"Fannie—" Jesse's earlier confidence slipped. "I thought you understood why I was doing this. If you want to take some of those books before Dave gets at them, you're welcome to. Take what you want. I don't care. I just want them out."

"I do want some of those books." Fannie looked helplessly toward the familiar old bookshop. "But why not let me buy it all from you? Why throw it away a box at a time like this?"

"You know why!" Jesse's gaze suddenly burned to life. "I don't want anything from my *daet*," he said, his voice lowered to a growl. "I don't want his advice, or his suggestions, or his lessons, or his business. I don't want any of it!"

But not everyone had the luxury of throwing an entire inheritance in the trash! Did he know how privileged he was to be able to do that? Because she had to find a way to support herself, or she'd be forced into a loveless marriage!

"What if I do?" she asked breathlessly. "What if I want what Caleb built?"

Jesse's expression darkened. "Then you don't understand me at all."

"So if I was your friend, I'd help you burn it to the ground?" she demanded.

"Something like that. *Yah!*"

"You know what?" Her voice shook. "I am your friend, and I will not encourage you in this. He's dead, Jesse! He's *dead*. He's facing Gott for what he did. He's either finding mercy with a penitent heart, or he's finding judgment. But that is in Gott's hands now!"

People had stopped to stare—Amish and English alike, and Fannie felt her face heat.

"Don't do this in the street," Jesse pleaded, lowering his voice.

Fannie had nothing else to say—she'd said it all, and now everyone was staring. She looked over her shoulder toward the chocolate shop, and she saw the lights on inside, and the door was cracked open.

So without another word, she fled, and the people in her path quickly stepped out of the way. She hauled open the door to Black Bonnet Amish Chocolates, then pulled it shut and locked it just as Esther Mae came out calling, "We're closed!"

Fannie stalked through the storefront and met Esther Mae at the swinging door that connected the kitchen to the rest of the shop.

"What's happened?" Esther Mae asked.

"It's a long story," Fannie said, but tears filled her eyes. "I don't even know why I'm this upset. I knew what Jesse was doing."

"What is Jesse doing?" Esther Mae asked, concern written all over her face. She went over to the front window and looked out. She wasn't going to see anything dramatic outside. The next group of passengers was climbing up into the wagon for their ride.

"He's selling Kauffman Books piece by piece. He's dismantling it," she replied.

"Oh…" Esther Mae looked less worried now. "All right. Well, he did inherit it."

"I know. I offered to buy the business, and he won't sell it to me."

"You have that kind of money?" Esther Mae asked in surprise.

"I have my part of the inheritance from my parents," she said. "So I do—for the right thing. I can't squander it."

"I'm not suggesting you would," Esther Mae said, softening her voice. "I just didn't realize you were looking to buy a business. I thought you were looking for another job."

"Another job would be helpful until I do find the right business to buy. I don't want to fritter the money away on just living," Fannie said. "There is no other place I want to spend every waking hour than a bookstore. And I can try and put one together for myself, but Kauffman Books was very special to me. I'd like to give it a new life."

"Did you tell him that?"

"Of course I told him that!" She rubbed her hands over her face. Was this really about the bookstore? Because Fannie wasn't sure anymore! *Yah*, she wanted to buy it, but her balance with her old friend was tipping again, and it shouldn't bother her this much.

"Isn't Jesse taking you driving, though?" Esther Mae asked. "I mean…he is courting you, *yah*? If he wants to be rid of the business, and the woman he's thinking of spending his life with wants to buy it, the two of you could just run it together."

Yah, Fannie could see how that looked. But Jesse was not considering her as a wife. This was all an act, and Fannie would not get any proper sympathy from Esther Mae, because she didn't know the truth of their relationship, either.

"We all grieve differently," Esther Mae added softly when Fannie hadn't answered, then she angled her head toward the kitchen. "Come make chocolates with me?"

That seemed like a safer solution by far.

Fannie nodded.

"I've made the ring box for the Englisher who is proposing to his girlfriend," Esther Mae said. "Come tell me what you think."

While other women were having romantic Christmases—an Englisher woman was going to receive a proposal, Miriam Yoder had her new husband and their baby girl, and all sorts of other married friends would be settling in with their husbands and little ones, too—Fannie had a fake courtship, and her emotions in turmoil.

This deal with Jesse was supposed to give her enough space and time to sort out her future, and so far, she hadn't done any proper planning.

"It's beautiful," Fannie said, looking down at the engraved box with the lid that fit perfectly on top.

"We just need to make the chocolates that surround it," Esther Mae said. "I was going to start with some mint cream dark chocolate diamonds."

It would be a lovely proposal for another couple. Fannie had to firm her resolve and figure out her own future. Jesse was not going to be part of her life in a meaningful way, no matter how much she wished he'd change his mind and stay.

That was it—that was the thorn that was sticking her so painfully. She wanted him to stay, and she already knew he wouldn't be swayed.

* * *

That evening, Jesse sat in his grandparents' kitchen, staring at his half-finished plate of food. His grandmother had made a delicious meal of beef Stroganoff, crusty bread and peach cobbler for dessert. The food was good—he knew that—but he wasn't enjoying it like he normally would. He'd really upset Fannie this evening, and he wasn't sure how. He wasn't in the wrong! He was simply taking care of his own personal business, and she'd erupted on him.

"I thought you'd be hungrier," Mammi said. "You've had a busy day. How was the festival?"

"Very festive," he said dryly. He didn't want to talk about the festival.

"Did you see any friends?" she prodded.

Jesse looked up to meet his grandmother's half-anxious gaze. She could sense something was wrong, and he was doing his best to pretend everything was fine for her benefit, but she seemed to sense that things were off.

"*Yah.* A few friends," he said.

"Just tell your grandmother what's got you bent out of shape," Dawdie said over his shoulder as he headed in sock feet into the sitting room. "You'll spare yourself three hours of questions."

Mammi shrugged innocently, and Jesse shook his head with a rueful little smile.

"Well?" Mammi urged.

"I think I had an argument with Fannie. I'm just not sure," he said.

"How can you not be sure?" Mammi asked.

"It didn't make sense. I found a buyer for some books, and she got upset."

Mammi nodded soberly. "It's not about the books, then."

Easy enough for her to say. But then, what was it about?

"I think it is about the books, though," he countered. "She really loved Daet's shop, and—" And he wouldn't sell it in one piece. He also wouldn't keep it. His grandparents were upset about the same things. He shouldn't bring this up.

"And?" Mammi asked gently.

"That's all." That's all he'd tell her, at least. "She loved the shop and she was upset I found a buyer for some books, I guess. She thought the books were worth more."

"Well, if there is one thing I've learned over the years, it's that when we jump to conclusions, we only make fools of ourselves. You're going to have to go talk to her. Are you driving her to work tomorrow?"

"She has the day off," he replied.

"Then I'd suggest you go over to her place and you ask her straight what's going on, because I can guess, and you can guess, but she's the one person who can tell you exactly what she was thinking. And then you'll know, at least."

Except, Fannie had gotten upset with him and marched off and left him standing in the street like a fool. If anyone should come find anyone, he figured it should be her. She knew what his *daet* had done to him. She knew why he needed to be free of that shop, and she still wanted it for herself. What did that say about her loyalties?

"Maybe," he said gruffly.

Mammi spread her hands. "In any relationship, Jesse, you have to talk."

She was probably right. He'd be irritable until he talked to her, anyway.

Fannie didn't come by the bookshop the next day. Jesse did pack up some books for Dave Morton, and he came with a cube van and picked them up. But Jesse didn't give him as many boxes as he'd originally planned. He didn't touch the Amish fiction section, the poetry and some of the tourist photography books that he thought Fannie might like. She might hate that he was emptying this place out, but he could give her some small piece of it.

Looking around Kauffman Books, he noted that most of the shelves were bare now. There was still the stash of receipt tape, the old till, handled paper bags with *Kauffman Books* printed on the side. There were a few old boxes in the back of the store he hadn't gone through yet, but Dave had cleared out fifteen boxes of books, and paid Jesse for them accordingly in cash.

There was something sad about this old store looking so empty, like a frail old farmer who used to be a beast of a man. Even the memories of this place felt feeble without the heavily laden shelves of books to bear witness. A lump formed in Jesse's throat.

When he was a little boy, his *daet* had given him a Christmas gift one year—a history of the Anabaptist faith. It was hardcover and cloth-bound. Inside, his *daet* had inscribed *Live up to your forefathers*.

Most of those forefathers had been killed for their faith, and Jesse remembered lying in bed as a child, staring at that book on his dresser and trembling with dread. There was no comfort from his *daet*. No explanations. And when he'd gotten up the courage to ask Daet if he thought they'd have to make that kind of sacrifice, his *daet* had said, "You'd better be ready and willing."

That was no comfort for a nine-year-old boy. And he'd had nightmares for years. He was already living in Indiana when a sermon had given him the comfort he'd needed all those years ago, but had never received.

"When Gott calls us to great sacrifice, it comes with great purpose and Gott's whisper sending us upon a great mission. He also provides superhuman comfort to his child, who must face that last step in such frightening times. Gott is a good father, and he knows we are but dust, and he strengthens us."

Gott was a good father, but Caleb was not. That book, complete with inscription, was in the bottom of the very first box he'd loaded up into Dave's cube van.

Gott, I don't know how to forgive my father...

The fire had died down in the potbellied stove, and Jesse shivered. He'd bring those boxes of books to Fannie, and maybe they'd work like a peace offering, and they could get back onto the same track again.

It didn't take Jesse long to load up the buggy with those few boxes of books, and then he hitched up and headed off down the street toward those familiar old country roads.

It was just after three when he arrived at the

Flaud farm, and the farmhouse had a pleasant little curl of smoke coming out of the chimney. Jesse tied his horse up at the hitching post, and then started unloading boxes onto the step. When he pulled the third and final box out of the back of the buggy, he saw the side door open and Fannie standing in the doorway, her shawl already around her shoulders.

"What are you doing?" she asked.

"You said these books were special to you," he said. "I put aside the ones I thought you'd like most."

She opened the top box and pulled out a little volume of poetry. She pulled it against her chest, and tears misted her eyes.

"*Danke*, Jesse," she said.

"It's nothing." He shrugged, but he was glad he'd hit on the right thing, after all. He carried the last box past her into the house and then brought the others inside as well, and stacked them against a wall. "Are they okay here for now?"

"*Yah*, that's fine," Fannie replied.

Fannie's *aent* Bethany was at the kitchen sink peeling potatoes, and she cast Jesse a smile.

"It's nice to see you, Jesse," she said.

Jesse pulled off his hat and scrubbed a hand through his hair. He looked over at Fannie, and she stepped a little closer so they could keep their words private.

"I'm sorry if I—" He sighed. "I don't know exactly what I did, Fannie. I'm just being honest. But if you tell me, I'll try not to do it again."

"It's hard to explain," she said, but her gaze flickered in her aunt's direction. It would be hard to explain in front of others, at least.

"Do you want to go for a walk or something?" he asked.

Did she want to get out into the cold, brisk wind and be able to talk openly—that was what he was asking.

"*Yah.*" She met his gaze and nodded. "*Yah,* I do."

"Meet me outside, then?" he asked. "I need to put the horse under the shelter."

A few minutes later, the horse was in the shelter with fresh hay and no wind, and Jesse and Fannie walked together down the drive toward the gravel road. This felt better to be alone with her. It was easier to talk with her when they didn't have everyone staring, and when they got to the road, he reached out and took her hand.

He wasn't sure why he did it, but it felt right to hold her a little bit closer, and she tightened her grip on his hand through their gloves, almost as if she felt the same way.

"I'm sorry I got so upset," Fannie said, breaking the silence between them.

"What were you so mad about?" he asked.

"I'm just going to miss you a lot," she said. "And I know what missing you feels like, because I've done a fair amount of it."

Jesse tugged her a little closer in response. "I missed you, too. I might not have communicated it well, but I felt it."

They both fell silent for a little while, their boots crunching along the snowy shoulder of the road.

"Can I ask you something?" he said cautiously.

"Of course."

Jesse exhaled slowly. "This matters to me, but it's delicate."

"Go on, Jesse," she said. "What is it?"

"How come, even after knowing what my *daet* did to me, are you so attached to the store he built?" he asked. "You know what he did. You know some of what I hid. You know enough, and I feel like you're choosing his side."

"I'm not," she said.

"I meant it when I said you should be helping me dismantle that place," he said.

"Your *daet* sat in that shop blaming himself for you leaving," she said. "Rightfully so, as it turns out. And I sat there missing you. But the comfort I found in that store didn't come from your father. It came from the books that he let me read on those shelves. I crumbled when you left, Jesse. I'm embarrassed to say it, because obviously you were fine. But I did. And those books helped me to find myself again."

"I'm sorry," he said quietly.

"It's okay. You did what you had to do, and I had to learn how to stop leaning on you."

He wished she could still lean on him, though. He wished that he could still be her tough friend who could lend her his strength. The thought of her leaning on anyone else hit the jealous part of his heart.

"You can lean on me while I'm here," he said, and gave her hand a gentle tug. She tipped her head against his shoulder, and he felt like he'd gained an inch of height in that moment. He did want to be her hero, and right now he wished more than anything that she'd come to Indiana—not as a pal. As more.

But before he could say anything, a buggy turned onto the road, and while Fannie did lift her head off his shoulder, he kept her hand tightly in his. The buggy approached, and Jesse spotted Dieter Glick in the driver's seat. He was alone—his *kinner* were not with him. He looked at Jesse and Fannie in surprise, seeming to take them in in one glance, and a sudden glow of understanding appeared in his expression. He met Jesse's gaze, then it flicked over to Fannie, and he felt her freeze.

Dieter turned his attention forward again, and didn't look at them again as he passed on by. They both turned and watched as he slowed to turn into the Flaud drive. He was on his way to visit Moe, it would seem.

"Oh..." Fannie breathed.

But Fannie shouldn't feel badly for this. She wasn't interested in Dieter, and he was being pushed on to her. It was good for Dieter to see that Fannie wasn't for him. He needed to know it so he could stop listening to her uncle insisting that she was interested when she wasn't!

"I think you've made your point, don't you?" Jesse asked.

Chapter Nine

Fannie watched the buggy disappear into the trees as it turned down their drive. She looked up at Jesse, her pulse speeding up.

"Why do I feel like I'm in trouble?" she asked.

"I don't know," he replied. "You shouldn't."

Right. She shouldn't. She knew that. She wasn't doing anything wrong. If she was courting Jesse, there was nothing wrong with it. She'd already been clear with her uncle that she wasn't interested in Dieter. Fannie hadn't done anything wrong!

And yet, that nagging feeling of having done something underhanded remained.

"Do you want to keep walking?" Jesse asked.

"Well, I certainly don't want to go back right now," she said.

Jesse gave her hand a squeeze and they continued on up the road together. The farther she got from home right now, the better. She didn't look over her shoulder, and instead leaned into Jesse's strong arm.

"Are you okay?" Jesse asked.

"*Yah*, I'm okay." She sighed. "He looked like he understood that you and I are—" She stopped. "He believed we're courting."

"*Yah*, he saw what we wanted him to see."

"I feel a little guilty, though," she admitted. "We aren't courting, Jesse. It's a lie."

And Fannie lived by honesty as a rule in her life. She didn't lie—not in word, and not by allowing an older man to court her whom she could never love.

"We never said we were courting," Jesse replied, his voice low. "And holding my hand— was that for appearances just now?"

She felt some heat in her cheeks. She'd been holding his hand because it was warm and comforting, and that physical connection between them felt like it was holding her up.

"*Nee*..." she said. It wasn't for appearances.

"I'm holding your hand right now because I want to," he said.

Her heart gave a tumble, and she didn't look up. "Me, too."

He tugged her a little closer against him as the wind picked up. She was grateful for her bonnet to both block the wind and to hide her face.

"You were always the happiest part of my days here in Menno Hills," he said. "You made me feel like I was important. I looked forward to our chats, and our walks, and our jokes together. You held me together."

Fannie had held Jesse together? She'd lived and breathed for him! She'd thought about him constantly. She'd been head over heels in love with this man, and then he'd just walked away.

"Fannie, say something..."

She stopped and turned, tipping up her face to look up at him, and she found his dark gaze searching hers. What did he want her to say? What could she say? There were moderate things she might not regret later, but nothing sprang to mind.

"You were my best friend, Jesse," she whispered, and she wished she was capable of finding something less deeply true to say, but she wasn't. "You were my everything!"

Not her boyfriend. Not her crush. He'd been the friend who saw her through thick and thin—the truest part of every day.

Jesse pulled her a little closer against him, blocking out some of that wind.

"I don't remember you being this pretty..." he breathed.

Fannie froze. Did he mean that?

"You shouldn't joke like that," she whispered.

"Who's joking?" He swallowed.

And suddenly she was filled with such a wave a loneliness that it nearly rocked her. He'd come back, and he'd filled up all those achingly empty parts of her heart all over again, and when he left again, it was going to hurt. But at least this time, he'd seen her, and he'd opened up. Dear, sweet Jesse. She'd miss him so much more than he ever knew.

Fannie rose up onto her tiptoes, and she only meant to kiss his cold-reddened cheek, but there was something about the way he turned his head and the way her stiff bonnet didn't allow for much maneuvering, because her lips didn't touch the sandpaper of his cheek—they connected with his warm lips.

She gasped, her heart skipping a beat, and instead of pulling back, Jesse's lips followed hers. He gathered her up against him in a warm embrace. For a moment, she wasn't sure what to do, and then her eyes fluttered shut, and she rested her hands against his chest.

She'd never kissed a man before, but somehow this felt just right—Jesse's arms around her waist, and their warm breath mingling under the shelter of her bonnet. When he pulled back, she blinked up at him, her heart pattering like a runaway horse.

"You kissed me," she said.

"I think you kissed me, Fannie," he countered.

Did he think that? Had she just kissed him? Her heart hammered to a stop.

"I thought I was kissing your cheek!" she said, and she took a step back.

Jesse laughed softly.

"Fannie, I was only teasing. I knew you wanted to kiss my cheek. I just—" He swallowed. "I've been thinking about doing that for days."

"You have?"

"Yah."

"I thought we were just friends," she said.

He angled his head to the side. "Maybe I was wrong about that. You're a whole lot more than a friend."

The words she'd longed to hear for years, and now Jesse was finally seeing the woman in her. But what did that mean now?

Fannie heard the creak of a wheel, and she spotted a buggy coming out of their drive, but it turned the opposite direction. Dieter was leaving, and he didn't want to pass them again. She felt a pang of remorse. She didn't want a romance with Dieter, but she couldn't help but feel she'd handled this badly.

"Are you okay?" he asked.

"I'm fine." She met his gaze with a smile.

Whatever had happened with Dieter, Jesse had just kissed her, and she wanted to memorize every detail.

"Ready to head back?" Jesse asked quietly.

She nodded. "Time to face my *ankel*."

"Do you want me to stay with you while you do?"

She shook her head. "I'll do it alone. It'll be fine."

They headed back down the road, but this time, Fannie felt a little stronger, a little more confident. Jesse's kiss had changed something inside of her, and she wasn't even sure what it was! She'd need to think about it alone and sift through her feelings, but she something had shifted, and she wasn't afraid to face Ankel Moe anymore.

She wasn't afraid to face Dieter, either.

Fannie looked up at Jesse, and he smiled shyly.

"Am I going to need to apologize for kissing you like that?" Jesse asked.

She shook her head. "Don't you dare."

And he squeezed her hand a little harder. Whatever this was between her and Jesse, it was real. There was no faking here, no keeping up appearances. It was honest and true—and maybe wouldn't even last—but today, she'd needed the reminder that her heart could truly skip a beat.

Mamm had been right about that. It was worth waiting for.

They walked the rest of the way back to the Flaud farm in silence, and Fannie let go of Jesse's hand when they turned down the drive. There was no use in flaunting their connection in her aunt's and uncle's faces, especially after what Dieter had seen. He would have told them, no doubt, and they'd be disappointed in her.

I didn't do anything wrong, she reminded herself. *Gott, give me strength.*

Fannie went back into the house as Jesse's buggy rattled off. She didn't think she could face a lecture from her aunt and uncle in Jesse's presence. It would be bad enough without Jesse witnessing the embarrassing moment.

In the kitchen, Aent Bethany was rolling out some noodles on the floured counter with her big, heavy rolling pin, and she looked up sadly as Fannie put her bonnet on the shelf by the door.

"Hello," Fannie called, hoping she sounded natural, but her aunt's pained expression didn't change. The lecture was coming. She could feel it.

Ankel Moe came over and helped her out of her shawl, hanging it up for her. Fannie eyed her uncle uncertainly at the surprisingly gentle gesture. She'd expected some anger on their end, not this strange sadness that had settled over the kitchen.

"Did you have a nice walk?" Aent Bethany asked.

"*Yah.* It was cold, but...nice." Fannie smiled uncertainly, waiting for them to say something—anything, really. She was ready for it now—braced for the worst.

"Are you hungry?" Aent Bethany asked. "I think we have some strudel in the cupboard."

"I'm not hungry," Fannie said. Her stomach was in knots.

"Fannie, we have some bad news," Ankel Moe said. "I'm very sorry about it, and I'm upset on your behalf."

Fannie blinked. Was this not about Dieter, after all?

"What's happened?" Fannie asked.

"While you were out, Dieter Glick came by," Ankel Moe said. "And he said he's no longer wishing to pursue anything further...with you."

The words were expected, but they still stung. Maybe it was the way Ankel Moe pronounced it like a death sentence, but she caught herself wincing.

"I'm sorry, Fannie," Aent Bethany said. "I know you weren't particularly interested in him yet, but we had hoped he might make a good, reliable husband for you once you saw more in him. There was no need to rush. And I think a man who thinks that a young woman should be chased into marriage is a man who doesn't understand women at all."

Her aunt was upset—on Fannie's behalf! Aent Bethany pressed her lips into a thin line and applied her irritation to the noodle dough.

"Who needs to rush a girl to marriage? Could he not have taken a few months? What kind of a fool would marry a man she hardly knew? It's the rest of her life she's considering!"

"It's okay," Fannie said. "It's not the end of the world. He's just a man looking for a *mamm* for his five *kinner*, and I'm not that *mamm*."

"You are a quality girl," Ankel Moe said. "I want you to know that. You are lovely inside and out. You have good character, and you're smart, too. You're well-read. You could easily teach school, let alone those little *kinner* of Dieter's! You *are* a quality girl, Fannie. Don't you let the passing interest of a man like Dieter convince you otherwise."

"I wasn't going to," Fannie said feebly.

"Good." Ankel Moe's face colored a little bit. "Fannie, I owe you an apology. I thought that he was the kind of man who would be stable and reliable. I thought that once he'd formed an interest in a woman, it would last. I hadn't realized he was the kind of man whose affection would be that changeable. But it seems that he isn't what we thought."

Except that Dieter Glick was a perfectly good man, she realized in a rush. He'd seen her walking with Jesse, and he hadn't said a word about it. He'd allowed Ankel Moe and Aent Bethany to think the worst of him, and he hadn't told them why he'd changed his mind. Dieter Glick was a very kind man, she realized.

"*Nee*, he's a decent man," Fannie said. "He really is. But I'm not old enough to raise five *kinner* yet, and I'm not the one for him. I know that for a fact, and I think he knows that, too."

"You are being very generous, Fannie," Ankel Moe said. "And that is to your credit. You will find the man for you. I know you will."

Fannie dropped her gaze, a lump in her throat. Her uncle and aunt weren't upset with her—they were defending her. They were deeply hurt that Dieter would reject her!

"Well," Aent Bethany said. "I think tonight for dinner, we should go get a burger. Or maybe a pizza."

"I don't know that I could handle going out tonight," Fannie said. And it wasn't because of Dieter's changed feelings, either. She had much to think over tonight, and she wanted the time alone.

"I'll go get a pizza to go from the place in

town," Ankel Moe said, and he patted her shoulder affectionately. "Extra cheese, the way you like it."

"That's a very good idea," Aent Bethany agreed.

And what could Fannie say? They loved her, and were trying to protect her feelings. And she loved them, too. Sometimes, that was expressed with pizza.

As Jesse drove back toward his grandparents' home, he exhaled a breath that hung frozen in the air in front of him.

"What did I do?" he muttered to himself.

He'd kissed Fannie—that's what he'd done! He'd kissed his best friend…and he'd meant it. That was the scariest part. He'd meant that kiss. Fannie was wonderful! She was sweet, smart, brave… And for a very long time, she'd been his in a pure and innocent way.

And he'd kissed her!

Jesse rubbed a gloved hand over his chin. The glove was cold, and he took hold of the second rein again. Kissing her had been very foolish of him, because it changed everything—for him, at least. He was leaving town after Christmas, and now, he was going to want to bring her with him.

But that wasn't going to be simple, was it?

Fannie had ties to Menno Hills, and she wasn't about to leave it all behind. She wouldn't accept his reasons, either. He was angry still at his father. He was bitter from a silent, secret upbringing that had scarred him. And Fannie wouldn't leave him with those feelings. She'd want him to forgive, to find a way beyond it, while all he wanted was an escape. Wasn't starting over just as good?

Not to Fannie.

Jesse sighed. He'd kissed her, and she'd kissed him back. That had been an honest moment between them, and even though he knew it was probably the most foolish idea he'd had yet, he wanted to do it again!

Fannie felt right in his arms, and he didn't want her in any other man's arms, either.

"I'd better stop that right now," he said aloud.

He was going back to Indiana, and she was staying here. She'd find a good man and marry him, and Jesse was just going to have to accept that.

Nothing had really changed, had it?

When he got back to his grandparents' home, Jesse thought he had talked some sense into himself, and he unhitched his buggy and put the horse into the stable. He was surprised to find Dawdie there. The old man was leaning against the pile of hay bales, and he had his Bible in his hands. He closed it when he saw Jesse.

"You're back," Dawdie said.

"*Yah*, I'm back." Jesse led his horse into the stall and shut the door.

"I went by the bookshop today," Dawdie said. "I thought you'd be there, but you weren't, I guess. I looked in the window. It's starting to look empty."

"I sold a lot of books to another bookstore," Jesse said.

Dawdie chewed on his bottom lip. "You really don't want to keep it?"

His grandfather was never going to understand this, was he? Jesse sighed. "I don't want anything from my father. Nothing at all."

"Why?" Dawdie asked, his voice low. "Just let me understand, Jesse."

And so Jesse explained. For the first time, he laid out the worst of it to his grandfather. He told him about the things his *daet* would do—the love he'd withhold, the punishment he'd mete out if Jesse made mistakes. Daet had wanted perfection. And the more he talked, the more he remembered. Until at last, he'd said all he needed to say. Dawdie pulled off his hat, revealing his bald head and wispy white hair.

"I'm sorry, Jesse. I was a coward. I didn't realize what he was doing to you, but I didn't force this issue, either. Caleb could have a sharp tongue with your grandmother and I, too, and I just did my best to keep the peace. It was wrong of me."

"I just wish I knew why he was so angry all the time," Jesse said. "If Daet had lived, I would have asked him that eventually."

"He was bitter," Dawdie said, and he cleared his throat.

"Bitter about me?"

"Bitter about life." Dawdie sighed. "Caleb had these high ideas. He thought I was a simpleminded man because I never built my farm up very much. I sold it, and your *mammi* and I lived off the proceeds in our old age, determined not to be a burden on our *kinner*. Your *ankels* all moved elsewhere, and your *daet* started up the feedstore. Your *aents* married and had their own families to worry about. Caleb was the one we should have moved in with when we got old, but…"

"But?" Jesse prompted.

"But we didn't think we'd be welcome. So we made sure we could keep ourselves."

"And what about this feedstore?" Jesse asked. "I never knew about that."

"It was before you were born," Dawdie replied. "First, there was a restaurant that failed. But restaurants are very difficult to make money off of. And then when the restaurant went under, he bought a feedstore. You see, your *daet* was convinced that if a man was just smart enough and tough enough, he could come out on top. The feedstore turned out to be much harder to turn a profit than Caleb figured it would be, and he got an offer to sell it. He got a little more out of it than he'd bought it for, which made it possible for him to start up Kauffman Books."

"Okay...so why was he bitter?" Jesse asked.

Because he could hear the truth in those words—his *daet* had been incredibly bitter. He'd been angry, exacting and cold.

"Gott didn't give him the life he felt he deserved," Dawdie said. "And he wouldn't listen to me. He said that if a man was just smart enough in business, he could have a nice fat bank account and never worry about the future, but that never happened for Caleb. All of his bright ideas barely made enough to keep him afloat. He made a decent living with that bookstore, but never enough to pad his bank account the way he wanted. And then he married your mother, and she got sick. He was angry about that, too."

"Daet was like that..." Jesse took the horse's water bucket and headed to the tap.

"He looked down on me, too," Dawdie said. "I wasn't a rich man, therefore he thought I'd been foolish. He was going to do better than I did."

Jesse turned off the tap and looked back at his grandfather standing there, with his stooped shoulders and watery eyes.

"You aren't foolish, Dawdie," Jesse said. "I promise you that."

"Well, my son thought I was," Dawdie replied. "He was going to prove me wrong. But Gott never promised us wealth. He promised us heaven. That's a very different kind of reward."

"I'm not living in Indiana hoping to get rich, Dawdie," Jesse said. "Just so you know."

"Good... I'm glad to hear that." Dawdie smiled faintly. "You make me proud, Jesse. You don't have to have a pile of money to make your grandfather deeply proud of you."

A lump rose in Jesse's throat. "*Danke*. I suppose I was a disappointment to my *daet*, though."

"Your *daet* was disappointed in himself," Dawdie replied. "He was wrong about a lot of things. He felt badly about it after you left, though. He told me that he might have been wrong about his child-rearing theories. That took a lot for him to admit."

"You had my address. You could have forwarded a letter from him," Jesse said.

"He never wrote one," Dawdie admitted. "I

asked him to. I pestered him to write to you. But I think he was ashamed. I didn't know why, but it makes more sense now. He missed you, and he regretted a great deal."

That explained some of the softness that Fannie remembered from his father—gentleness that he'd never experienced from his *daet*. And standing in this stable with the smell of hay and manure, he was reminded of the stable where Jesus was born—brought into a broken world with broken hearts and broken families, and he'd been born to save them from their sins and from themselves.

"I'm doing my best, Dawdie," Jesse said. "And when I go back to Indiana, it isn't because I'm angry with you. I just need something that's mine. Not Daet's. I hope you understand."

Dawdie looked at him sadly. "I do. I just wish I could make it better."

But it wasn't Dawdie's wound to heal. All the same, even though Jesse knew what Gott required of him—to forgive—he wasn't sure he could do it from here.

Chapter Ten

The next morning, Black Bonnet Amish Chocolates was busy with Christmas shoppers. Outside, a Santa Claus was ringing a bell, collecting money for the food bank. The Santa was very English, and Fannie would never quite understand the Englishers' way of celebrating Christmas. The Amish didn't ring bells and dress up in costumes. If they were raising money for a local need, they simply went door-to-door and humbly asked for a donation. The Amish way was quieter and more discreet.

And across the street, Fannie could see Kauffman Books. Jesse had driven her to work this morning, and they'd both been a little shy. The fact that Dieter had told her uncle that he was no longer interested in a romantic relationship with her had been on the tip of her tongue, but she'd been afraid to say it. It would end all of this—the pretend courtship, the rides to work together, the extra time in each other's company.

And she hadn't been ready for that yet, so she hadn't said anything. More secrets. This wasn't who she was...

"Fannie, would you take over for me making chocolates with Iris?" Esther Mae asked, bustling back out into the store front again.

Fannie rose from where she'd been restocking some stick candy canes, and carried the box of candy with her back toward the kitchen.

"Of course!" she said.

"*Danke*, Fannie," Esther Mae said.

Esther Mae liked to keep a finger on the pulse of her business, as she put it. This was the sort of business acumen that Fannie should pay attention to. She slipped into the kitchen and found Iris coating some hedgehog molds with milk chocolate.

"Good morning, Fannie," Iris said with a smile.

"Good morning." Fannie put on one of the big, white, wraparound aprons to protect her dress. "What can I do?"

"The hazelnut ganache needs to go into the piping bags," Iris said.

Fannie went to the gas-powered fridge and pulled out the ganache, already made the night before. She knew this job well, and she fetched a plastic piping bag, along with a plain nozzle.

"How are things going?" Iris asked.

"Oh...fine." She smiled. But was it fine? She and Jesse hadn't spoken about their kiss this morning. She hadn't told him about Dieter's decision. That wasn't a sign of all being fine.

"You sure?" Iris cast her a sympathetic look. "How is Dieter?"

"He's fine, too, I think," she replied, but her voice shook just a little.

"He's really nice, Fannie. You don't need to be nervous of him."

"We aren't going to make a couple," Fannie said. "He won't be courting me any further."

"Oh, that's just fear talking now," Iris said. "Let me give you a little tip. I happen to know that his very favorite candies are butter mints. He used to love them when we were in school, and that kind of taste doesn't change. So, why don't we put together a little box of some chocolates and butter mints, and you can bring them to him? Maybe as a Christmas gift. I think it would do the trick."

It was a very sweet image, but Fannie wouldn't be the woman to bring that box of treats.

"*Nee*, Iris," Fannie said. "He isn't interested in me anymore. And that's a good thing! I can't become an instant mother to five *kinner*! And... he's much older than me. I can't...be a wife to him."

She looked at Iris pleadingly, and Iris's cheeks colored.

"Oh!" she said. "Oh...*yah*, I understand that."

There was more to marriage than housework, after all. But Dieter was a very decent man. He hadn't said a word about what he'd seen to Fannie's aunt and uncle, and he'd been nothing but kind and respectful to her. In fact, he'd taken any bad opinion onto himself in order to spare her embarrassment. Perhaps, being so much older, he understood. He'd had romance before with his first wife. He knew what it felt like. Perhaps Fannie owed Dieter a good deed in return.

"But Dieter did talk about you very nicely the one time we visited properly," Fannie said. "I think he talked about you most of all."

"Me?" Iris stared at Fannie, and the chocolate she was pouring overflowed the mold.

"Iris!"

"Oh dear..." Iris saved what chocolate she could, and went to the sink for a rag. When she came back, her attention was fixed on the cleaning up, but she said, "What do you mean, he talked about me?"

"About how you were very good friends," she said. "He liked you very much. I think, Iris, that if anyone should bring a box of chocolates and butter mints to Dieter, it should be you."

Iris's face blazed, and she turned her back to bring the cloth to the sink again. She stayed there, rinsing the cloth under the tap longer than necessary.

"Iris?"

Iris turned then. Her face was still red.

"You think he's very nice," Fannie said. "You knew him when you were in school. He thinks you were very nice, too..."

Iris shook her head.

"If he was interested in me, he might have said something," Iris said. "I'm not the kind of woman men trip over themselves to court, you know."

"Maybe he thought if you were interested in him, you would do the same," Fannie said. Then she sighed. "I don't know, Iris, I'm no expert in romance."

"Neither am I, obviously," Iris replied.

"Well...one thing I do know is that Christmas is a very romantic time of year," Fannie said. "Think of that Englisher who is proposing to his girlfriend. It's a time for family, and hope, and happiness. And when we think of those things, we often think about the person we want to share them with, too."

Iris nodded. "I know I do."

"Me, too." Fannie's Christmases were getting lonelier as the years went by. And the last two

Christmases without Jesse had been worst of all. When everyone around here was celebrating in their family units, and Fannie didn't have a husband or a *bobli*.

"He needs a wife, Iris," Fannie said earnestly. "And he told my *ankel* plainly that he isn't interested in marrying me."

Iris's gaze clouded.

"Oh, don't feel badly for me!" Fannie said. "I'm fine, Iris! I am. Think of yourself. Those five adorable *kinner* need a *mamm* to take care of them. And I dare say, Dieter needs a wife to take care of him, too."

"And you're sure he doesn't want to court you?" Iris asked.

"Positive."

A smile touched Iris's lips. "Do I dare bring him something?"

"Bring enough for the *kinner*, too," Fannie said. "They'd love a treat, I'm sure."

"When should I go?" Iris breathed.

"After work, of course!" Fannie laughed. "Iris, he likes you already very much! I told you, at my home, he talked about you most of the time!"

Iris nodded. "I'm going to do it."

"Good." Fannie nodded to the chocolate mold. "We should chill that."

"Yes!" Iris startled herself back into work.

Dieter deserved a woman who'd love him well, and so did his *kinner*. But with Dieter's mind changed, Fannie had to be honest with Jesse, too. Fannie was not a secretive woman by nature, and she did not want to become one. It was time to put everything out in the open.

"Where did you come from?" Jesse squatted down to pet an orange cat that twined around his ankles. It had snow on its fur, so it had been outside, but how did it get in?

He looked around the shop. He hadn't found any cat supplies—no litter box, no food or bowl... And he certainly didn't smell any litter. Did his father have a cat in here? The animal slipped away from his fingers and disappeared into the back room.

The shop wasn't quite so empty as it appeared through the front window. He'd emptied out the nonfiction sections of books, but there were a lot of books left. Should he call Dave Morton and see if he wanted to take more?

Jesse needed this place emptied, but he'd found more school supplies, a pretty large selection of lined journals, some pens of different colors and uses. His *daet* had collected all sorts of extras around here that Jesse had never seen before, but he could imagine them selling well—if they were put on display, that was.

Why was he even thinking about sales? He didn't want to sell this stuff! He wanted to be rid of it! And yet, after his talk with his grandfather, his emotions were in a tangle.

Daet had been a deeply flawed man, but it was starting to make sense now. Before, it had just seemed so cruel and random, but at least now he could see what had driven his father to such bitterness.

Jesse looked around himself. His *daet* had done well. He'd built up a business for himself. Jesse might not want it, but his *daet* had been an Amish success. Hadn't he?

But he'd wanted more. More than this business could provide, more than the community could give. He'd wanted money and status—what could be less Amish? Nothing had been enough.

"Gott, why wasn't I enough?" That was the thought that stabbed deepest. Other parents he knew found satisfaction in their *kinner*, but Daet never had. He'd only been disappointed, no matter how hard Jesse tried to do well.

There was a tap on the door, and he recognized it immediately. Fannie had come by. He hadn't been sure if she would or not after that kiss yesterday, and he couldn't help but smile. She was the bright spot in this visit—the one person who felt like a sigh of relief.

He opened the door, and Fannie came inside with a rush of swirling snow.

"Work is done for the day?" he asked.

Fannie nodded. Outside, the day was dimming, and Englisher vehicles had their headlights on as they drove down the street. Light glowed from inside the chocolate shop, and the door opened, people emerging, others entering. The holidays were always busy.

"You smell like chocolate," he said.

Fannie smiled at that. "I always smell like chocolate."

She was dismissing the observation, but he liked that aroma. That sweet smell seemed woven right into her clothes these days, lingering in her *kapp*, too. He'd noticed that when he had kissed her yesterday.

"How was your day?" he asked.

"Busy. I was in the kitchen a lot, making chocolate hedgehogs and chocolate-covered cherries," she said.

"Did you bring me any samples?" he asked with a teasing grin.

"No, I did not," she said, lifting her chin. "Esther Mae doesn't just send chocolate home with us. She sells it."

"I'm only joking," he said, although he wouldn't have turned it down. Today had been a strange, emotionally charged day, and he felt like he could use something sweet to refuel.

"Besides, Iris is going to bring Dieter some chocolate tonight."

"Oh?" He looked over at her in surprise. "I thought you weren't going to do any more seed planting?"

"Just one more seed," Fannie said with a twinkle in her eye. "I think they'd make a good match. She's the one he should be courting."

"Do you need me to take you driving again?" he asked.

Fannie stomped snow off her boots on the mat and slipped past him toward the woodstove.

"Actually, Dieter is not trying to court me anymore," she said, her back turned.

"*Nee?* So seeing us walking together was enough?" he asked.

"It was. He told my *ankel* that he was no longer interested."

Jesse was silent, processing this information.

"And he was downright decent about it." Fannie turned then, and he saw emotion flooding her eyes. "He didn't tell my *aent* and *ankel* that he'd seen us holding hands. He didn't say a word. He just told them that he'd changed his mind, and my *aent* and *ankel* thought the worst of him for that. The worst! And he took that bad opinion on himself in order to not tell on me. On us."

"That was downright decent of him," Jesse murmured.

"I know!" Fannie shook her head. "If he'd told them the truth, they would have lectured me about appearances, and about being careful around you, and I don't even know what all else. But they didn't. They felt terrible for me, because they think he just changed his mind."

"Do you kind of like Dieter more for that?" Jesse asked. He wasn't sure what he wanted to hear, but he'd better face the truth.

"Not romantically, Jesse." She rolled her eyes. "But I think you were right that he's a good man, and he deserves a good woman to raise those *kinner* with, and I think Iris would be perfect for him. So when she told me that Dieter used to like butter mints, thinking that I could bring some for him, I encouraged her to do it instead." Fannie shot him an exultant smile. "And if they marry, I want credit!"

"From who?" Jesse asked with a low laugh. "You can't bring up that he was trying to court you. It would be in bad taste."

"From you, maybe." Her cheeks pinked. "I want you to tell me I was the one to make that happen."

"All right..." He liked the way she smiled when she was pleased with herself.

Outside the window, he saw Iris Bischel come

out of the store, a Black Bonnet bag in one hand, and her purse over her shoulder.

"She's leaving now," Jesse said.

They both watched her disappear around the corner, likely going to get her horse and buggy from the stable behind the shops, and they were silent for a few beats. Jesse was glad to see another woman slipping in to take Fannie's place. The thought of Fannie with Dieter, nice as he was, made his blood boil. Call it old-fashioned jealousy, but he was glad that Iris was going out to bring him chocolates.

"So..." Fannie turned back toward him. "It's over."

"What's over?" he asked.

"Our arrangement," she said. "You don't have to pretend to court me anymore—the danger is past."

Jesse frowned. "And you think that's what this is?"

Fannie stilled. "I'm just trying to be honest with you. I didn't tell you on the way over—"

"Why?" he asked. "Why didn't you tell me?"

"Because—" Her cheeks flushed. "Because I wasn't brave enough. Is that what you wanted to hear? I was a coward, and I didn't want to end it all just then. But I'm not going to hide it from you, or from anyone. Dieter is now certain he doesn't want me, and I can focus on my own future."

"Do you think that I've been spending all this time with you just to keep up appearances?" he demanded.

"*Nee*, not exactly." But she wasn't looking entirely sure of herself now, and he wished he could open her eyes and make her see it!

"Crackers in a barrel, Fannie!" he exclaimed. "You're my best friend! Of course, I'd help you...and even if I weren't trying to chase off some farmer for you, I'd still want to see you, to talk to you, to listen to what you think, and—" The words got caught in his throat, because he couldn't put it all into language for her.

"You don't think I should have told you?" she asked.

"Of course, you should have told me!" he said. "Fannie, who else would you tell? Who else would understand the way I would? Who else would be this pleased with you for being fair and kind and still managing to get your way? Huh? Who?"

"No one," she said with a low laugh.

"Exactly." He caught her hand in his and tugged her closer. "We never talked about what happened yesterday, but I meant what I said. I'm here with you because I want to be."

He wasn't sure what it was—the way she

looked up at him with those wide, mildly surprised eyes, or just that intoxicating scent of chocolate that always seemed to cling to her—but something had changed since he'd come back to Menno Hills. Maybe he had changed...

"And the kiss?" she asked hesitantly.

How was he supposed to explain that? He couldn't. But he'd been thinking about that kiss ever since, and he'd been wishing he could do it again.

The cat came sauntering out of the back room again, and it brushed past his leg, purring. He wished he could explain it—how his feelings for Fannie had grown somehow, and deepened. How Fannie was exactly what she'd always been, except a little wiser now, and a little deeper, more herself. And that changed everything...somehow...

The cat twined around his ankle again, and he sighed in frustration, bent down and picked the cat up.

"Where did you come from, cat?" he demanded, and then he turned back to Fannie in irritation.

"Fannie, I can't explain that kiss! I can't... I kissed you because—" And he slid one hand behind her neck, tugged her in and pressed his lips over hers once more. She leaned against him, and it was like his whole heart wrapped around her in that moment. And then he knew. He knew exactly why he'd kissed her, why he'd been spending all of this time with her... Why he couldn't stop thinking about her...

When he pulled back and looked down at her, her hands pressed against his chest in a way that made him want to drop this cat and kiss her all over again, he said, "I kissed you because I love you, Fannie."

And then the cat squirmed out of his one-handed grip, and dropped lightly to the ground.

"What?" Fannie breathed.

Jesse's eyes were filled with tenderness, and he touched her cheek gently, but he didn't repeat himself.

How long had she waited to hear those words? She'd pined for Jesse for years before she'd finally made her peace with simply being his best friend. At least she was closer to him than anyone else in Menno Hills!

"I have loved you for so long," she whispered.

That had been too honest, and she felt her cheeks heat. But it was true! She'd loved him with everything she had had, even when she didn't think there was any hope of him loving her back.

"But do you love me still?" he asked miserably. "Because you used to love me, and I'm not the same man anymore. I'm not the boy you grew up with. Do you love me now, as I am?"

She nodded. "Of course, Jesse."

"*Yah?*" His eyes shone, and he swallowed hard. "Come to Indiana with me."

His words hit her like a blow. He was still leaving? Her heart thundered to a stop. He would still go back, even after declaring his feelings for her?

"Go to Indiana?" she repeated.

"*Yah*, come with me."

But something about that solution didn't feel right, either. He still wanted to leave everything that had grown them into the adults they were. He wanted her to leave her roots and stability behind. And he wanted her to do it on a feeling.

"Jesse, you could stay in Menno Hills."

"I can't," he said. "You know why. But your *aent* and *ankel* are going to be moving soon. You don't have anything solid right now for your future plans—"

"Jesse, I'm not going to move with a man who isn't my husband," she said.

He was silent.

"Besides," she added in a gentler tone. "You might love me, but I'm not going to fix what's broken inside of you. I couldn't, even if I tried. You're angry, and bitter, and you have every right to it! But if I went with you to Indiana, you'd soon discover that having me there with you didn't fix it. I'd just be a Band-Aid for a little while. And then my reputation would be unsavable."

"You've thought this through," he said quietly.

"I think ahead." She swallowed hard. "Jesse, you *could* stay…"

But she knew he wouldn't. He had too much bitterness here, but that bitterness wasn't going to stay in Menno Hills. He'd carry it with him, and sometimes he'd almost forget about it, but it would never really go away. Who was to say she wouldn't be a constant reminder of Menno Hills and his upbringing? She'd been his best friend for all of those years!

"Do you really think I'd just stop loving you if you came with me?" he asked sadly.

"I think that things would change," she said.

"I could court you properly out there."

"Jesse, you have no idea how tempting that is," she said quietly. "I want nothing more than for you to court me, but I also know you very well, and…you're angry. I understand it, but you have to find your own answers, or else it will poison what we have between us, too. It already drove you away from me once, Jesse. What's to say it won't happen again?"

Jesse wrapped his arms around her and pulled

her against his solid heartbeat. She leaned her cheek against his shirt, sadness filling her up. He wouldn't stay. And she couldn't go. What could they do?

"I still love you," he whispered.

"Me, too..."

She pulled back. She couldn't stay here with her heart breaking. There was no solution.

Looking around the shop, she could see the big gaps on the shelves from the books he'd already sold, and the boxes from the back room standing in a haphazard pile. This shop would be torn apart and given away, just like their friendship.

It wouldn't last. There was no going back to what they were, and even before they'd spoken of any feelings, it hadn't been enough to keep them together.

"I need to go home," she said, her voice shaking. Because there was one thing she was certain of—her *aent* and *ankel* would be there for her, to comfort her and remind her that life would keep moving forward.

Tomorrow was Christmas Eve, and there would be plenty to do to prepare.

"I loved this shop, Jesse," Fannie said, and a tear slipped down her cheek. "I loved it because it was filled with books, and stories, and hope. And I loved it because it was connected to you.

When you came back, I imagined looking up and having you march through that door, and I wouldn't miss you coming home again."

"Dismantling this place isn't going to erase my hard memories, is it?" he asked miserably.

"*Nee*, I don't think it will."

"I already sold the nonfiction books," Jesse said, and he looked around himself. "But there's still a lot of books here."

"I'm sure you'll figure it out," she said. "But find some way to honor this place, Jesse. It was here for me when I needed it. It deserves some sort of respectful send-off, if only for that."

Jesse was silent, and Fannie wrapped her shawl more tightly around her shoulders, heading for the door.

"Fannie," Jesse said, and she looked up at him again.

"*Yah?*"

"Do you still want to buy the shop?" he asked, his voice tight.

"Do you mean it?" she asked.

"*Yah.* Chopping it up into little pieces isn't going to change anything. Maybe it'll be the solution you need, and I can help provide it."

"I'd—" Tears welled in her eyes. "I'd be honored to run this shop."

"But change the name," he said gruffly. "*Fannie's Fiction* has a nice ring to it."

"Or you could stay..." she whispered.

He swallowed hard. And she could see the battle on his face. Would he choose forgiveness and healing?

"We'll sort out the details," he said at last. "I'll sell it to you cheap. But it's yours."

He couldn't stay, and she even understood. But no woman was going to heal that wound in his heart, and she didn't want him to discover that sad truth while he was holding her love. It would crush her completely.

"*Danke*, Jesse."

"Can I drive you home?" he asked.

Fannie shook her head. If she stayed another moment, she was going to sit down and cry, and she would not do that in front of Jesse. She'd wrap her heart around this shop later, but right now she just needed some solitude.

She pushed out into the cold winter evening, and the bell above the door tinkled merrily as she hurried down the sidewalk, fighting back tears. She'd go sit in a coffee shop and ask the owner to call her a cab. It would be an expensive ride home, but at least there wouldn't be anyone she knew to watch her cry.

Jesse Kauffman just kept breaking her heart again and again. You'd think a girl would learn.

Chapter Eleven

Jesse put another piece of wood into the stove, and he sank down onto a stool. How had it all crumbled so quickly? But maybe he deserved it, too. He'd ignored her for two years. He'd focused on his own anger and pain, and he hadn't once picked up a pen to tell her anything he was thinking and feeling. He'd been immature and foolish, and self-centered. That was the truth of it. Why should she trust that he'd be anything different now?

Except that he was. He loved her, and if she came to Indiana, he would well and truly court her. He never wanted to be parted from her again.

"Gott, why didn't I see what a treasure she was sooner?" he prayed aloud.

Because Fannie truly was a treasure. He hadn't exactly been blind to her good qualities, but he'd certainly been blind to her feminine nature. She'd just been a friend before. A pal. How could he have been so oblivious?

Jesse heard a tiny mewling sound, and he turned to see the orange cat padding back into the storefront, a ball of fur in her mouth. It was a tiny white-and-orange kitten, and the cat placed the kitten on the tiles in front of the stove, and then flopped down next to the little thing in the spreading warmth.

"You have a baby..." Jesse said softly, and his words caught in his throat. He had no idea where this cat had come from, or why she'd chosen him to introduce her kitten to, but he felt the holiness of the moment.

The kitten snuggled up next to its mother, and they both closed their eyes. Was this cat a mouser? She looked plump enough, and he hadn't seen a single mouse or dropping since he'd arrived.

He'd make a little bed for her in the back room, and make sure she had a dish of water. If there was no room at the inn, so to speak, he'd make some room for her here. Fannie would do something good with this shop, and maybe passing it along to her could redeem this old place somehow, give it a new life with new purpose.

There was a tap on the window, and he looked up, hoping to see Fannie, but it was his grandfather. Dawdie stood out there in the falling snow, his black had pressed down on his head and his shoulders hunched up against the cold. He had a bundle in his arms.

Jesse sighed. All he wanted was some time by himself, some solitude to try and sort out his own layers of grief, but it didn't look like he was going to get that tonight. He pushed himself to his feet and went over to open the door for his grandfather.

"Hi, Dawdie," he said tiredly.

He stepped back, and Dawdie shuffled in. Snow dusted the tops of his shoulders and had gathered on the top of his hat. He pulled off his hat and knocked it against his leg, hoisting the package in his arms a little higher.

"Is something wrong?" Jesse asked.

"*Nee*, nothing is the matter," Dawdie replied. "You didn't come home."

Jesse was also a grown man who was only visiting. He wasn't a boy anymore, needing to be supervised or checked on. But he smiled wanly and led the way toward the stove in the center of the shop.

"Come warm up," Jesse said.

Dawdie put his package onto the counter, and then stretched his hands toward the heat. He looked down at the cat and kitten.

"You have company, do you?" Dawdie asked.

"Looks that way," Jesse replied.

"Where is Fannie?"

That was the question, wasn't it?

"She didn't want me to drive her home," he replied. That was the simplest true statement he could say.

"What did you do?" Dawdie asked with a frown.

"Me?" Jesse asked. "Why do you think I did something?"

"Because she's been in love with you for years, and now you're back in town spending time with her. And suddenly she doesn't want a ride home? I think you hurt her feelings."

"I told her I love her."

Dawdie blinked.

"*Yah*..." Jesse smiled bitterly. "I told her I love her, and she feels the same way about me, but it won't work."

"Why not?" Dawdie asked.

"Because she won't go with me to Indiana, and she thinks she won't make me happy."

"Hogwash." Dawdie shook his head. "You'd be blissfully happy with that woman. She's a catch."

"Tell me about it," Jesse muttered. "I'm well aware. She doesn't trust me, Dawdie. I haven't been the reliable kind of man she needs up until now, and I don't think I blame her."

"You're a good man," Dawdie said.

"I'm a damaged man, Dawdie."

Dawdie turned back to the counter and slowly unwrapped the package that he'd brought with him.

"What's that?" Jesse asked.

"An early Christmas gift," Dawdie said. "I was going to give it to you on Christmas morning, but I had a feeling you might need it more tonight. Call it a nudge from above."

It seemed that Gott was sending in some reinforcements tonight—the cat, the kitten and now Dawdie. No matter how alone he felt, Gott was still working, but what he was working on, Jesse couldn't say. Because all he wanted right now was to see Fannie again, and she'd already made her feelings clear.

Dawdie hoisted up the big, leatherbound German Luther family Bible, and Jesse stared at his grandfather, stunned. It was two hundred years old! The binding was starting to disintegrate, and the pages were yellowed with age. Dawdie only read from this Bible on special occasions, not wanting to damage the delicate pages.

"Dawdie, what are you doing?" Jesse asked.

"I tried to give this Bible to your *daet* after your *mamm* died, and he refused it," Dawdie said. "I tried again after you left, and he refused it again."

"He refused it?" Jesse accepted the heavy book from his grandfather's soft hands, and he looked reverently down at the leatherbound cover.

"That Bible has been in our family for a very long time," Dawdie said quietly. "I always meant to give it to the next generation to be kept safe and passed along again."

"Why didn't my *daet* want it?" Jesse asked.

"He said he wasn't worthy of that task—continuing a family tradition of that weight," Dawdie said.

It was Jesse who Daet didn't think was worthy of that Bible, because Daet could have easily taken it for him. That old feeling of shame and insignificance descended on Jesse again.

"Why me?" Jesse asked dismally.

"Because you're my grandson," Dawdie said. "And I think you'd treasure it."

"I will, *yah*." Obviously, he would!

"Jesse, you are not only your father's son," Dawdie said. "Do you know that?"

"What do you mean?" Jesse put the heavy Bible onto the counter. He opened the cover and looked down at the faint, spidery handwriting that covered the inside endpaper. The births and deaths had long ago spilled over from the few pages that had been included in the original Bible.

"You come from a long line of believers," Dawdie said. "There is a crowd of witnesses in heaven right now, and you are related to them. You're my grandson. You're my children's nephew. You have cousins, and friends, and others in your life, and you mean something to each of them. You are not just your father's son."

Jesse frowned. "Okay..."

"I should have been a better father myself," Dawdie said. "I missed the signs. I somehow didn't get through to Caleb about the things that mattered most. I didn't realize what he was doing to you, either. I blame myself."

"Dawdie—"

"*Nee*, I do," Dawdie insisted. "Caleb was my little boy, once upon a time. He was my responsibility." Dawdie sighed. "Jesse, I understand you not wanting to keep this shop. It was all your *daet* could leave to you, but I understand the burden of it, too. So, I just want you to know that while you can sell this shop, you still belong to us. You're still my grandson. There will always be a place for you when you come to visit. Always."

"*Danke*, Dawdie," Jesse said, his throat thick with emotion.

"These are just walls, Jesse," Dawdie said. "That's all they are. Just walls."

"I wish that was all they were," he said. "They're my childhood, too, Dawdie."

His grandfather nodded slowly. "I understand, but don't let the pain of your childhood ruin the rest of your adulthood. You have many, many more years, Gott willing, and you have more years ahead of you than you have behind you. Forgiveness isn't because your father deserves it. None of us deserves it. It's because you deserve a life of your own."

Dawdie's gaze moved over the shelves—some emptied, some still full. There was sadness in his eyes. Caleb had been his son, and while Jesse's memories of this shop were tainted, he could imagine that his grandfather's memories of this shop would be different. This was his son's business effort that succeeded. Dawdie would have been proud of this place that bore the family name. Dawdie was a Kauffman, too, after all.

The cat stood up, stretched and came over to rub against Jesse's legs. He looked down at her—an affectionate animal that seemed to want to comfort him.

"Dawdie, what do I do about this cat?" Jesse asked.

"That's your *daet*'s cat," Dawdie replied.

"How come you left her here?" he asked.

"Oh, she chose your *daet* more than he chose her. She came and went when she wanted to. Somehow, she always found her way in."

Dawdie gave him a warm smile. "Take your time, Jesse. But remember that your grandmother will wait up. She worries like that."

As if Dawdie hadn't worried. Jesse nodded sadly.

"I won't be too long, Dawdie."

His grandfather headed back out into the cold winter night, and Jesse locked the door after him. Then he went to that the big family Bible, and he opened those front pages again. He found the record of his father's birth, the record of his marriage, the record of Jesse's birth...

This Bible was witness to two hundred years of Anabaptist believers, and it did make him feel better to realize that. He wasn't only his father's son.

And yet, deep inside of him, he still felt the nudge against his conscience. He needed to forgive. Fannie wasn't wrong about that. Somehow, he had to find a way to forgive his *daet*, even if he did it from Indiana.

As Fannie came in the door that evening, her aunt bustled her inside and bumped the door shut after her. The older woman smelled like Christmas baking—cinnamon and gingerbread. Aent Bethany always made faceless gingerbread people each Christmas—the men in hats and the women in aprons. They were perfect couples, and even before Fannie's parents had died, she'd loved those cookies. They reminded her of Amish families—husbands and wives who loved each other. It was all she'd ever really wanted out of life when she was a girl, but she'd never dreamed that loving each other wouldn't be enough. Life was so much more complicated than children realized.

Ankel Moe wasn't in the room, which was probably for the best. Fannie allowed her aunt to take her shawl off her shoulders.

"You hired a cab?" Aent Bethany asked. "Why? I thought Jesse was driving you home."

"It's okay," Fannie said. "I was able to pay for it myself."

It wasn't exactly an answer to her aunt's question, but it was the pertinent information, as far as Fannie was concerned. Her aunt and uncle didn't need to worry about paying for it.

"I'm less worried about the money than I am about what went wrong." Aent Bethany hung up Fannie's shawl on a peg. "I have your dinner in the oven, by the way. Roast chicken."

"I'm not hungry."

Aent Bethany stilled, her brown eyes meeting Fannie's. "Did you eat already?"

Fannie shook her head. She wouldn't be able to eat even if she tried. Her stomach was in a knot.

"Come sit with me," Aent Bethany said.

Fannie was filled to the brim with tears and emotion, but she couldn't deny her aunt a moment at the table. She nodded, and swallowed back tears.

Aent Bethany pulled a chair close to Fannie's, and they both sat down.

"Now..." Her aunt folded her hands. "Start at the beginning, dear."

"I don't know what to say," Fannie said, and a tear escaped and trickled down her cheek.

"Jesse?" Aent Bethany asked gently.

"*Yah.*" Fannie nodded and her lips wobbled. "I love him..."

And she told her aunt everything—how she had asked Jesse to spend time with her so that her family would stop pushing her toward Dieter Glick, and how all the feelings she'd stored up for Jesse had just started to grow. Except, he returned her feelings this time.

"So what's the problem?" Aent Bethany asked.

"I can't just leave Menno Hills behind—not the way he'd want me to," Fannie said. "He hates it here. He has too many hard memories with his *daet* who was being abusive when no one else was watching. And he can't stay—he can't return. He wants to just wipe this place from his heart and move on. Can I go along for that? Can I move to Indiana to court a man who would never come back to our hometown?"

"Is that all?" Aent Bethany asked. "He might bring you back to visit for you own sweet memories here."

"I'm not his solution, Aent Bethany," Fannie said. "I loved him for years, and now that he's back in town, I'm a distraction. That's what I am. He's working through his anger and bitterness, and I'm a happy part of Menno Hills for him. But that's all I am."

"You are more than that, dear girl."

"I am, but I don't think I am to him," she replied. "I'm a comfort, but Gott created me to be more than a Band-Aid for a man's emotional wounds."

Aent Bethany was silent for a moment, then she nodded. "I understand that. I do."

Fannie wiped a tear off her cheek. "He said he'll sell me the bookstore—what's left of it. And I can make a life for myself with it. I can support myself, and build it back up."

"Or you could come to Florida," Aent Bethany said gently.

"No, I can't," Fannie said. "My heart is here—broken as it is. And I can help others with a bookstore—I can put the right book into the right hands. I can have a good life on my own, Aent Bethany."

"On your own?" Aent Bethany shook her head. "Fannie, can I tell you something that I learned?"

Fannie nodded.

"Gott is a *gott* of comfort. He meets us in our most terrible times, and he gives us that peace that passes understanding. But Gott is also a *gott* of solutions and answered prayers! We will see the goodness of Gott in the land of the living. He leads us through green pastures and beside still waters. He will give you the desires of your heart, Fannie. You're afraid of being alone, so you are trying to prepare for the worst—ending up alone. But you could change your perspective and have faith that Gott will give you the best!"

"The best was Jesse," she said, her throat tight.

"Not if he doesn't love you like you deserve to be loved," Aent Bethany said, disagreeing. "You have loved him with all your heart for years, and you deserve a man who will love you back just as much."

When Fannie was in Jesse's arms, it did feel like he loved her just as powerfully as she did him... But feelings could be deceptive. And Fannie was more than just herself—she was part of this community, and she couldn't walk away from the home where her parents lay resting.

If Jesse was looking for comfort, she knew that she wouldn't be enough, and it would hurt more to go to Indiana and watch him drift away from her than it would hurt to face reality now.

"I'll run a bookstore," Fannie said. "It will support me—" She stopped, remembering her aunt's wise words. "It will support me until Gott brings me together with the right man. But even then, whoever marries me could run it with me. And we can bring joy to Menno Hills for years to come."

Ankel Moe appeared in the doorway, his dark gaze filled with sadness. He'd heard—it was evident by the look on his face.

"I would have felt better leaving you with a husband," Ankel Moe said.

"I need the right one," Fannie said. "I need the freedom to find him."

Ankel Moe nodded. "You will, Fannie. You're a wonderful young woman—kind, smart, thoughtful. You're going to find a good man who will love you properly, but don't you settle for less than that."

Fannie nodded, not trusting herself to words.

"You'll do well in business," Ankel Moe added. "You've got a good mind for it."

Her uncle's vote of confidence did make her feel better. There was still Gott's goodness in her life, and she would find it.

That night, though, Fannie crawled into bed, and her tears soaked into her pillow. Gott's goodness was out there, but tonight she needed his comfort. Because she loved Jesse even more than she had before. And she now knew what it felt like to have him love her in return.

But a future with him still wasn't possible. What would happen to her if she went to Indiana, just to have Jesse change his mind? Or worse, what if he married her out of obligation after tarnishing her reputation, and she went the rest of her life chasing after her own husband's heart, and never quite reaching it?

This Christmas would be a painful one where she watched other couples and their *kinner* enjoying the celebration of Jesus's birth. But she would take comfort in Gott's goodness, despite her broken heart.

"Oh, Gott, if only Jesse could have been mine," she wept. "I would have loved him well..."

If only.

Chapter Twelve

Jesse slept terribly that night. He tossed and turned, and when he finally drifted off out of pure exhaustion, he dreamed of Fannie. Except, it was Christmas, and he was trying to give her a present, but she couldn't hear him and wouldn't turn around. Then he dreamed that he was running, and he could hardly move his feet. It was pure frustration, and he woke up in a sweat.

Today was Christmas Eve, and the truth was, he did want to see Fannie, but he wasn't picking her up for work this morning. That part of their relationship was over, and that might be for the best, considering that he wasn't sure he could be alone with her in the buggy. Not with his heart cracked in two. But he needed to bring her the key to the shop. At least that way, she could start arranging things the way she wanted them. And maybe then he could see her once more at the chocolate shop.

Maybe she would have changed her mind about going with him to Indiana... Was that too much to hope? He knew it was, but there was a part of his heart that just didn't want to give up on Fannie. Now that he knew how he felt about her, he couldn't close that door again. He was just hanging here like a gate swinging in the wind, in love with her, and with no hope.

Jesse waited until Black Bonnet Amish Chocolates would be open, and he drove into town.

He'd been praying all morning—that hurt, heartbroken kind of praying where a man didn't know what to ask for, but needed some sort of direction. He wanted to do something—fix this! But he couldn't force her to trust him, and he couldn't stay here, either.

He reined in his horse outside the chocolate shop, and then he looked over at Kauffman Books. The shop was dark and silent, and there was something about that sign that still poked at old scars. This store was not a place of happy memories for him, but if Fannie took over and changed it completely, maybe she could chase out those shadows in his absence.

Is this why I needed to come home, Gott? he prayed. *Was it to pass this store on to Fannie?*

Something was starting to feel right about Fannie taking over the store—so long as she tore down that Kauffman sign and put up something distinctly hers. Maybe Gott was leading for Fannie's blessing this Christmas, and that would have to be enough.

Jesse hopped out of the buggy and tied the horse to the hitching post. He gave the horse a reassuring pat before he headed up onto the sidewalk and into the chocolate shop.

The air smelled sweet in Black Bonnet Amish Chocolates, and there were a few customers looking at some gift items on shelves—chocolate arrangements wrapped in cellophane. Esther Mae was talking to an Englisher couple at the front counter, and her face was wreathed in smiles. Jesse could overhear a little bit of their conversation.

"I couldn't wait," the man was saying. "I was going to ask her at Christmas, but I couldn't put it off that long."

"He brought me a box of chocolates," the woman said, looking adoringly up at the Englisher fellow. "And I had no idea! I actually started eating one of the smaller chocolates, and he insisted I open the big one."

"And you said yes, of course!" Esther Mae said.

"I said yes." She laughed softly. "Do you want to see the ring?"

"Of course, I do!" Esther Mae said.

It appeared that these two had gotten engaged, which was perfectly nice for someone else, but their happiness tugged at his own wounds this morning. What made other couples work out when he and Fannie didn't? Why couldn't their love be enough?

He tried to look into the kitchen. Fannie must be working in the back today. Esther Mae and the young couple were chattering about summer wedding plans and some chocolate table centerpieces.

"We made up a little engagement announcement, and thought you might like one as a keepsake," the young man said.

More chattering, then they had to go—and another customer took their place to pay for a chocolate gift basket. Jesse turned and watched the Englisher couple go out the door. They leaned toward each other, and it was like the whole world existed just to swirl around them.

Did they know how hard it was to get a love like that, and have it turn into a lifetime together?

Don't let me get bitter, Gott, he prayed.

But he had to wonder how Fannie had slept last night.

"Hello, Jesse," Esther Mae called, and he realized that she'd served her last customer, leaving them alone in the shop for the moment.

"Good morning," Jesse said. "I was hoping to talk to Fannie."

"Fannie isn't working this morning," Esther Mae said. "She wasn't feeling well."

"Is she sick?" he asked.

"Just really sad." Esther Mae gave him a sympathetic look. "She left a message on my answering service. Thankfully, Iris could come in and help me out today."

So it was Iris in the back, and Fannie was at home. He couldn't just go by her uncle's home. Moe would be furious, no doubt. He'd told him not to do this to her again, hadn't he?

"Are you all right, Jesse?" Esther Mae asked.

"*Yah.*" He dropped his gaze.

"I think you're fibbing." The older woman came out from behind the counter and looked up into his face affectionately.

"Fannie is the one who deserves the care," he said.

"What happened?" Esther Mae asked. "I guessed that things ended between the two of you, but I don't know why."

So he explained it the best he could. Jesse loved Fannie, and she loved him, too, but she wouldn't leave Menno Hills with him, and he couldn't stay. He wished Fannie understood the pain he carried with him, and she did, but she had roots here, and she didn't trust that he'd love her for the rest of his life.

Esther Mae nodded slowly. "But you do love her?"

"More than anything."

"Maybe it will just take time," Esther Mae said sadly.

"Maybe." But he knew Fannie better than that. Once she'd made her mind up about something, she wouldn't be wishy-washy about it. "I wanted to give Fannie the key to the shop. She's going to buy it from me for a good price, and I wanted her to have the key now so she can go inside and start arranging things the way she wants them."

He swallowed hard.

"It's kind of you to sell it to her," Esther Mae said. "She's at home right now."

He shook his head. "I won't be welcome there. Would you give her the key?"

"Sure." She accepted it with a nod, and then she looked up at Jesse pleadingly. "Jesse, don't give up."

"I think I have to," he replied softly.

"You two make such a good couple, though," Esther Mae said. "I have an eye for these things."

Jesse felt some heat in his face, and he dropped his gaze. The little engagement announcement caught his eye—it looked like a quick, homemade thing. But there was a Bible verse at the bottom of the paper that drew his eye. *Proverbs 19:14.* He didn't know the verse off the top of his head, but he was curious what verse would be meaningful to that happy couple. Call it morbid curiosity in the face of his own heartbreak.

"I'd better head out," he said. "*Danke,* Esther Mae. Tell her—" He stopped.

"Tell her what?" Esther Mae asked.

"Tell her I love her," he said, his voice gruff. "Even if she'll never be mine."

"Jesse, I won't wish you a Merry Christmas," Esther Mae said quietly. "But I will wish you a meaningful one. May Gott be your strength and comfort, and may you find his star and follow it. There is always a pinprick of hope."

It was a beautiful blessing, one that he knew would be of comfort this season. Maybe he'd be like a wise man, on a journey of his own.

"*Danke.*" He wasn't sure what else to say, so he gave her a nod and headed for the door. Christmastime had never been easy for Jesse, but this was going to be the most painful Christmas yet.

By the time the afternoon rolled around, Fannie wasn't sure if staying home from work had been the right thing to do. She'd been afraid that she'd go into work and just cry her eyes out. That wouldn't have been helpful to anyone…

But staying home with Aent Bethany doing the Christmas Eve cooking and cleaning hadn't been easy, either. Aent Bethany sang Christmas carols as she worked, and Fannie couldn't join in. The lump in her throat wouldn't allow it.

Nor did hard work scrub the pain out of her heart.

I love him, Gott, she kept praying.

Because she did! She'd loved Jesse for years. Would next Christmas be easier? Would she have gotten over the worst of her heartbreak by then? She'd gotten over her broken heart once already, and she knew that she could do it again. With time, and with Gott. But she did love him...

"Fannie, get that sweetbread out of the oven for me, would you?" Aent Bethany called.

Fannie got the oven mitts and opened the oven door. The scent of sweet lemon-cranberry loaves filled the house, and Fannie pulled them out, one at a time. They were nicely browned—complete Christmas perfection. And all Fannie wanted to do was sit down and cry.

The timing was miserable. Everyone around her wanted to be happy and to celebrate the holiday—of course, they did! And Fannie couldn't find any Christmas spirit inside of her.

There was a knock on the side door, and Fannie froze. It could be anyone—people dropped by on Christmas Eve...but all the same, her heart skipped a beat. Would it be Jesse coming by to see her?

She pulled out the last loaf and put it on top of the stove, then shut the oven door with a clang. She pulled off the oven mitts and hurried to the door.

"Merry Christmas, Fannie!"

Iris stood there with her shawl wrapped tightly around her, her cheeks pink from the cold and a smile on her face. She wore a dark red dress and a black apron that looked so vivid against the snow behind her that she almost looked like another woman. Fannie had never seen Iris sparkle quite this much before.

"Merry Christmas," Fannie said, hoping she didn't sound disappointed. "Come in."

"I can't stay long," Iris said. "Esther Mae sent me with this key for you. Jesse dropped it off."

But Iris did step inside into the warmth, and they shut the door behind them. Fannie turned the key over in her palm. She recognized it immediately. It was the store key.

"Is it for the bookstore?" Fannie whispered.

"*Yah.* It looks like he's selling it to you after all?" Iris asked.

"*Yah,* he said he would." She tried to smile, but wasn't sure she managed it.

"That's wonderful," Iris said. "It really is. I

know how much you love that shop. What a great Christmas gift to you."

A Christmas gift. Not long ago, Jesse agreeing to that sale would have seemed like a gift from above, a gift for her future, but now, it felt hollow. She wasn't thinking about her future right now. She was wondering what Jesse had been thinking.

"He dropped it by the shop?" Fannie asked, her voice shaking. He couldn't even come and give it to her in person? Because he knew where to find her.

"*Yah*, that's what Esther Mae said." Iris didn't seem to understand the import of that detail.

Was Jesse just that hurt? Or had his hurt turned into anger now? She wasn't sure she could face that.

"Fannie, it's a big secret, but since you were part of bringing us together, I wanted to tell you..." Iris's eyes sparkled.

"You're engaged to Dieter, aren't you?" Fannie asked, and she found that she could smile for her friend's happiness, after all. It was a small smile, but a sincere one.

Iris nodded. "We had a quiet talk, and he asked if I would marry him. We won't wait long. Those *kinner* need me sooner than later, and… and I don't want to wait any longer than I have to, honestly."

"I'm sure he feels the same way," Fannie said.

"*Yah*, he does." Iris sobered. "*Danke*, Fannie. *Danke* from the bottom of my heart. You are such a generous and unselfish woman, and I pray that Gott blesses you over and over again for helping me and Dieter to come together like you did."

"Oh…" Fannie felt some heat in her face. She didn't feel like she deserved quite that much credit.

"I mean it," Iris said earnestly.

"I'm just glad you're happy!" Fannie replied.

"I am happy!" Iris leaned over and gave Fannie a squeeze. Fannie shut her eyes, hugging her friend tightly. Of all the women in Menno Hills, Iris deserved this happiness.

"I have to get going," Iris said, pulling back. "Dieter is expecting me. I'm going to be cooking with the *kinner* this evening—we're baking cookies."

"That sounds wonderful. When is the wedding?"

"Next week."

So soon! But when a couple knew, they just knew, and Iris and Dieter were right for each other. Fannie might have nudged Iris in his direction, but that was all she'd done. If only it were that easy for her and Jesse.

"I'll see you later," Iris said. "Merry Christmas again!"

Fannie stood in the door until Iris drove away, and then she shut it slowly.

Merry Christmas, indeed. She was glad that Gott was providing for her friend, and may he listen to Iris's prayer and bless Fannie. But there was only one foolish, heartsick prayer inside of her. She wanted a way forward with Jesse.

But how could she trust Jesse's love to last this time around? Or would she simply have to trust Gott if he said no?

Chapter Thirteen

Jesse's grandparents had gone to visit a family member, leaving the house in warm quiet, and Jesse sat on the edge of the bed upstairs. Dawdie and Mammi would be home shortly. They were only dropping off some baking.

He'd felt right about selling the store to Fannie. It would help her, would give her a proper income. And knowing Fannie, she was smart. She'd build that place up into a thriving business, and who knew? Maybe he'd visit again one day and see Fannie's Books, or Fannie's Fiction, or Flaud Books—whatever she called it—filled to the rafters with books and customers alike, and he'd know that he'd helped her get her start.

Except, even that felt like heartbreak, because if he visited and saw Fannie's store, he'd also see Fannie's husband and *kinner*. He'd see the life that she'd chosen over coming to Indiana with him.

He might have understood her not wanting to move out to Indiana without being married. Courtships were important, but it would be a risk for her. The silly thing was, if he thought she'd come along with him, he'd be willing to marry her in a heartbeat, skip the courtship and make it legal.

That thought sped up his heartbeat. Just marrying her—it would solve almost everything... except she loved Menno Hills, and her parents were buried here. She didn't want to leave it behind, and while her love and most precious memories remained here, his deepest pain was nestled in right next to it.

Jesse ran his hand over that old family Bible his grandfather had given him. Dawdie had said that he wasn't just his father's son, and he'd been thinking that over. It was oddly comforting to think that he belonged to more people than just his parents. That thought had been soothing that aching, bleeding part of his heart that his father had wounded over and over again during his childhood. Jesse wasn't just Caleb's son.

Falling in love with his best friend had been a terrible idea, and yet all around him there were people falling in love, getting married... Like that Englisher couple. He'd been envious of their happiness—the way the young woman had looked up at her fiancé. They'd get to plan their life together, and move forward as a couple. Did they know what a blessing that was?

Proverbs 19:14. That was the verse on their announcement. He still didn't know what the verse said, and he carefully opened the old family Bible, and he turned the crinkling pages to the Book of Psalms, and then flipped past it to Proverbs.

He found the verse and ran his finger under the words as he read.

House and riches are the inheritance of fathers: and a prudent wife is from the Lord.

Jesse sat there in silence, his heart closing around the words. Jesse wasn't only Caleb's son, and while his *daet* had been able to leave him a bookshop, not every blessing in Menno Hills came from his *daet*.

And suddenly, it all came together in his mind so perfectly that tears sprang to his eyes. His *daet* had been a terrible parent, *yah*, but Jesse was more than Caleb's son. He was Gott's son, too. And his heavenly father had been giving him gifts where his earthly father hadn't been able. Gott had given him Fannie as a friend and a ray of sunshine in his life many years ago... Some things—like a sweet, noble, insightful woman—came from Gott!

Leaving Menno Hills wasn't going to clear out the pain, but Gott could. And suddenly, he knew that forgiving his flawed father would be a whole lot easier now that he could plainly see that his heavenly father had been leaning close and blessing him all this time.

Jesse had never been alone, and Gott had even provided him with the best gift a man could possibly receive, aside from salvation.

He grabbed his wallet, and headed out of his room and down the stairs. It was Christmas Eve, and Jesse knew what he had to do. He had to prove to Fannie that she wasn't just his comfort, she was his everything. And he thought he knew how.

Fannie stood at the counter with her aunt, decorating those perfect gingerbread couples. She was using blue royal icing for the woman's dress, and white for her apron and bonnet. Fannie's experience in chocolate making at Black Bonnet Amish Chocolates with Esther Mae had given her a steady hand, and Aent Bethany said she was better at it than she was.

"I remember these cookies from when I was little," Fannie said. "I loved them."

Aent Bethany smiled. "I know. One year I almost didn't make them, but I remembered how you'd lit up when you saw them the year before, so I made sure I had some just for you."

Fannie gave her aunt a misty smile. That was

back when her parents were alive. This Christmas, Fannie was missing them a lot.

"We have a guest," Ankel Moe said, looking out the window.

"Oh?" Aent Bethany picked up another cookie. She was decorating the men in gray pants and white shirts, with perfect loops of suspenders. They wore tan-colored hats—summer wear, not winter, but it looked prettier on a cookie.

"It's—" Ankel Moe's lips pressed together disapprovingly. "It's Jesse Kauffman."

Fannie startled and she put down her tube of icing. "It's Jesse?"

"I don't think he has any business here anymore," Ankel Moe said irritably. "Hasn't he done enough?"

"Oh, let him in," Aent Bethany said. "If Fannie wants to see him, that is."

"*Yah*, I do," Fannie said quickly.

Ankel Moe opened the door and gave a gruff hello, then stepped back. Jesse came inside, stamping the snow off his boots as he entered. He was carrying a cardboard box in one arm, and he gave Moe a respectful nod.

"Merry Christmas," Jesse said.

"Merry Christmas," Ankel Moe replied, but his tone was less than merry.

"Hi, Jesse," Fannie said, and she wiped her hands on her apron.

"You can talk in the sitting room with Fannie, if you like," Aent Bethany offered.

Jesse met Fannie's gaze, and he smiled then. "*Nee*, but *danke*, Aent Bethany. What I have to say, I need to say in front of the people who love Fannie most." He put the box down on the corner of the kitchen table. He still wore his boots, and Fannie wondered about the melting snow, and what her aunt would think.

"What do you need to say?" Fannie asked hesitantly.

"I love you," Jesse said.

Aent Bethany and Ankel Moe exchanged a look, but Fannie couldn't help but smile. Fannie crossed the kitchen and stopped in front of Jesse. It was wonderful to have him here, to just be next to him again.

"I know that," she said. "What else?"

"You don't trust that I'll keep on loving you," Jesse said quietly. "But I will. You think you're just comforting me during a difficult time, and that's all my feelings are, but I need to show you something."

He reached into the box and pulled out a little lamb made from a toilet paper tube and cotton balls. He tipped it so she could see inside, and she spotted her own name written there.

"I made that..." she breathed. She was remembering now. "What grade were we in? Third?"

"Second, I think," he said. "We traded lambs because we were best friends, remember? I brought yours home, and you brought mine. In the second grade, you were my everything already, Fannie. My *daet* didn't care about my crafts, but you did."

Fannie felt her eyes mist over. She'd kept his craft for years until it had fallen apart. It had been Jesse's...everything from Jesse had meant the world to her.

"And this—" He pulled out a bit of knitting. It was terrible knitting—all dropped stitches and picked-up stitches... It was red, and looked unfinished, even though it had been cast off the needles.

"Your first scarf," Jesse said. "You didn't have the patience to finish it."

"I remember that." She smiled. "Somehow, I remember it looking better."

"What?" He looked down at it. "I loved this. You'd made it."

"Your chest warmer," she said, suddenly remembering.

"*Yah.* It was soft and warm, and made by your hands, Fannie." He sobered. "I put it under my pillow and slept with it there for a long time. I lost it in a major house cleaning, and I found it in a box with the crafts I'd made, and the lamb you had made—tucked away by my *daet*."

"Why did he keep it?" she asked.

He shook his head. "I don't know, but I'm glad he did. Fannie, you think I'll stop loving you, but I won't. I was dealing with a lot in my childhood, and I didn't know that this soft, warm, protective feeling I've had for you all these years had a name. But I do now. I love you, Fannie. I always have, and I always will. I need you to know it, and I need your *ankel* Moe and *aent* Bethany to know it, too."

Jesse looked toward her aunt and uncle, then dropped his gaze to Fannie again.

"And I understand why you don't want to go to Indiana, so I won't go either. I'll stay here."

"You will?" Fannie whispered.

He nodded. "I want to be clear. Kauffman Books will end, and I want the bookstore with your name across the front of it. Unless you want to turn it into something else. I don't care. But we have to do it together. Because I can't run my *daet*'s store, but I can certainly run Fannie's Books with you."

"You'll really stay?" she asked, tears glistening in her eyes.

"*Yah*," he said. "And I said before, I wanted you to come so I could court you."

She nodded.

"Fannie, I want to marry you. Whatever it takes. That's what I want. I want to start a home with you, and I want to have *kinner* with you."

"What about your hard memories here?" she asked. Because that was a problem for Jesse.

"Memories follow a man around," he replied. "But I think I've found my way to forgive my *daet*...to start forgiving him, at least. I have a feeling it'll take a decision daily to set aside my anger."

"How?" she asked.

"I'm not only my father's son," he replied with a shrug. "I'm Gott's son, and my *dawdie*'s grandson. I'm your best friend, and if you'd have me, I'll be your devoted husband, too. Gott was providing for me all those years by giving me you. I don't have to define myself by my father. I have more than that to show me who I am. You were my everything, Fannie, and I was too angry and broken to see it. But I see it now, and if you'll give me a chance, I'll prove it to you every single day for the rest of my life."

"I love you, too, Jesse," Fannie said, and Jesse gathered her up in his arms, but stopped short of kissing her.

"Will you marry me, then?" he asked.

Fannie looked over at her aunt and uncle, who stood staring at them wide-eyed.

"Would we have your blessing?" Fannie asked.

Tears welled in Aent Bethany's eyes, and Ankel Moe muttered something and looked away uncomfortably.

"Go on, then," Ankel Moe said. "If you're getting married, you might as well kiss her, and we'll sort out some details."

Fannie looked up at Jesse, and he grinned down at her.

"*Yah*," she whispered. "I'll marry you."

Jesse gave her a gentle kiss on her lips—it was all they could do in front of her family—but she could feel all of the love bound up inside of him. Later on, when they were alone, she intended to fall into his arms and let him kiss her breathless.

"Merry Christmas, Fannie," Jesse said softly.

Her gaze moved down to the gingerbread cookies of those perfect Amish couples. Maybe they weren't perfect so much as made for each other. And all of the Christmas joy suddenly flowed into the room around them. That's right—it was Christmas!

"Merry Christmas, Jesse."

Epilogue

Christmas Eve was busy, and happy, and filled with secret plans for a wedding they weren't telling anyone about yet, besides just their closest family. Jesse's grandparents were thrilled about the news, and they'd offered to build a *dawdie hus* addition on their farmhouse so that Jesse and Fannie could live in the house and have some privacy, and they could move into the addition.

Fannie's aunt and uncle were quick to forgive Jesse for his past mistakes when they saw how much he truly loved their niece, and they immediately began wedding planning for that spring. It would be a big to-do, and they wanted to see Fannie properly married before they left for Florida.

Christmas Day was equally busy with visiting, eating, celebrating. And then, on Second Christmas, the day after Christmas Day, Jesse and Fannie headed into town. The shops were all closed up tight. They wouldn't open again until December 27, and then they'd all shut down again for Old Christmas.

They unlocked the door and headed into the shop. Jesse took a few minutes to stoke up a new fire in the potbellied stove. When he looked up, he found Fannie with a wistful look on her face.

"What do you want to change first?" Jesse asked.

"I want to paint the shelves white, and the walls, too," she said. "And we could move the cash register to the other side of the store, so that the best light is here—" She waved her arms. "And I want there to be room around the central stove so that people can sit in chairs around it and read."

"It sounds really nice," Jesse said. "You can do anything you want."

"I mean, we'd have to talk about it," Fannie said.

"Nope," he said with a grin. "I mean it. You can do anything you want with this store. When I come into this shop, I just want to see you."

"Then, I want to have a book club here," Fannie said. "We could order the book into the shop and the members could buy the book, and then they'd come and discuss it around this stove. It would be wonderful!"

"I agree," he said.

"And authors might come sign their books here—some might. I know we're a small town and we're out of the way, but once we built up a reputation for being a good shop, we could attract them."

Jesse leaned against the wall, watching the ideas light up her whole face. She was beautiful like this—happy, engaged, excited. And he wanted to make sure that she stayed this way. She'd have the bookstore, and he'd have her. Seemed like an easy enough solution now.

"What about when we have *kinner*?" he asked.

"We could hire an employee," she said. "If I've learned anything over at Black Bonnet Amish Chocolates, it's that there is always a worthy young woman or young man who needs the work. And somehow, Gott brings them along just when everyone needs it most."

"Sounds good to me," he said.

"Does it really?" Fannie asked. "This will be our family shop, our family legacy—yours and mine. I want you to be part of it."

"I am part of it," he said. "I'll be running it with you, won't I?"

"Will you really be happy this way?" she asked.

Jesse gathered her up in his arms and looked down into her gray eyes. Would he be happy? There was no other way he could possibly be happy. She was his everything, and Gott had given him a chance at something truly special by bringing Fannie into his life.

"*Yah*," he said simply.

"That's it?" she asked with a laugh. "*Yah?*"

"*Yah.* So long as I get to marry you." And he dipped his head down and covered her lips with his. She sighed and leaned into his arms, and it was like the bookstore and the street outside, and even the chocolate shop across the street swirled around them.

This was a new start, where Jesse and Fannie properly belonged to each other.

Fannie pulled back, breaking off the kiss, and she looked up at him.

"Fondest Fiction!" she said.

"What?"

"That's what we should call it," Fannie said. "I don't want to name it after me—it's ours. But we could call it Fondest Fiction. Because it all started with our love. What do you think?"

He grinned, pulled her back against him and let his kiss be his answer.

The rest of their lives was starting right now.

* * * * *

Dear Reader,

Thank you so much for choosing this story to read. I know you have choices, and when you choose my books, I'm honored. If you enjoyed this book, you might want to check out the other books I've written. There is a complete list on my website at PatriciaJohns.com.

If you'd like to enter giveaways and keep up with my book releases, you can also sign up for my newsletter. The link is on my website, too.

If you'd like to find me on social media, I'm always thrilled to hear from my readers. Reach out, and you'll make my day!

Patricia

Get up to 4 Free Books!

We'll send you 2 free books from each series you try PLUS a free Mystery Gift.

FREE Value Over **$25**

Both the **Love Inspired®** and **Love Inspired® Suspense** series feature compelling novels filled with inspirational romance, faith, forgiveness and hope.

YES! Please send me 2 FREE novels from the Love Inspired or Love Inspired Suspense series and my FREE gift (gift is worth about $10 retail). After receiving them, if I don't wish to receive any more books, I can return the shipping statement marked "cancel." If I don't cancel, I will receive 6 brand-new Love Inspired Larger-Print books or Love Inspired Suspense Larger-Print books every month and be billed just $7.19 each in the U.S. or $7.99 each in Canada. That is a savings of 20% off the cover price. It's quite a bargain! Shipping and handling is just 50¢ per book in the U.S. and $1.25 per book in Canada.* I understand that accepting the 2 free books and gift places me under no obligation to buy anything. I can always return a shipment and cancel at any time by calling the number below. The free books and gift are mine to keep no matter what I decide.

Choose one:
☐ **Love Inspired Larger-Print** (122/322 BPA G36Y)
☐ **Love Inspired Suspense Larger-Print** (107/307 BPA G36Y)
☐ **Or Try Both!** (122/322 & 107/307 BPA G36Z)

Name (please print) _____

Address _____ Apt. # _____

City _____ State/Province _____ Zip/Postal Code _____

Email: Please check this box ☐ if you would like to receive newsletters and promotional emails from Harlequin Enterprises ULC and its affiliates. You can unsubscribe anytime.

Mail to the Harlequin Reader Service:
IN U.S.A.: P.O. Box 1341, Buffalo, NY 14240-8531
IN CANADA: P.O. Box 603, Fort Erie, Ontario L2A 5X3

Want to explore our other series or interested in ebooks? Visit www.ReaderService.com or call 1-800-873-8635.

---

*Terms and prices subject to change without notice. Prices do not include sales taxes, which will be charged (if applicable) based on your state or country of residence. Canadian residents will be charged applicable taxes. Offer not valid in Quebec. This offer is limited to one order per household. Books received may not be as shown. Not valid for current subscribers to the Love Inspired or Love Inspired Suspense series. All orders subject to approval. Credit or debit balances in a customer's account(s) may be offset by any other outstanding balance owed by or to the customer. Please allow 4 to 6 weeks for delivery. Offer available while quantities last.

Your Privacy—Your information is being collected by Harlequin Enterprises ULC, operating as Harlequin Reader Service. For a complete summary of the information we collect, how we use this information and to whom it is disclosed, please visit our privacy notice located at https://corporate.harlequin.com/privacy-notice. Notice to California Residents – Under California law, you have specific rights to control and access your data. For more information on these rights and how to exercise them, visit https://corporate.harlequin.com/california-privacy. For additional information for residents of other U.S. states that provide their residents with certain rights with respect to personal data, visit https://corporate.harlequin.com/other-state-residents-privacy-rights/.

LIRLIS25